Lady Grace

Lady Grace

EVERY ERA HAS ITS FALLEN WOMEN

BY

Vicki Hopkins

DEDICATION

In memory of my second cousins (twice removed) who lost their lives in World War I:

- Private Thomas Douglas Holland: Killed in Action June 5, 1915 – Gallipoli, Turkey (18 years of age from Salford, United Kingdom. Buried in Helles Memorial Cemetery, Gallipoli, Turkey)
- Private Harry Walton: Killed in Action February 6, 1917 – France (42 years of age from Salford, United Kingdom. Buried in France)
- Private Gilbert Hough: Killed in Action October 9, 1917 – Belgium (18 years of age from Salford, United Kingdom. Buried in West Flanders, Belgium)
- Private Frederick John Holland: Killed in Action May 8, 1918 – France (27 years of age from Tuakau, New Zealand)
- Major George Henry Holland: Killed in Action May 15, 1918 – France (32 years of age from Tuakau, New Zealand. Buried in

Colincamps, Somme, France)
- Corporal John Holland Sapsford: Killed in Action November 4, 1918 – India (24 years of age from Prestwich, United Kingdom. Buried in Rawalpindi, Pakistan – formerly India)

In memory of the husbands of my first cousins (twice removed) who lost their lives in World War I:

- Sergeant Mark Kennedy: Killed in Action July 1, 1916 – France (32 years of age from Lancashire, United Kingdom. Buried in Thiepval Memorial, Picardie, France)
- Private Charles Edward Hurst: Killed in Action September 9, 1916 – France (26 years of age from Prestwich, United Kingdom. Buried in Thiepval Memorial, Picardie, France)
- Private George Wheeldon: Killed in Action October 5, 1918 – France (22 years of age from Manchester, United Kingdom. Buried in Vis-en-Artois British Cemetery, France)

In memory of my great-aunt's husband:
- Sergeant Henry Lofthouse: Died of wounds May 1, 1917 – Kent, England (30 years of age. Buried in Shorncliffe Camp, Kent, England)

-Rest in Peace-

TABLE OF CONTENTS

CHAPTER I

A WORLD TURNED UPSIDE DOWN

As a young woman of twenty-one, I did not think it outlandish to marry a man of forty. My reserved personality had never been an admirable quality that drew many suitors nor did I ever consider myself a romantic at heart.

Olivia, my dearest friend and confidante, held loftier notions of meeting a man who would sweep her off her feet. She daydreamed of passionate interludes with a charming husband. As entertaining as her aspirations had been, I made it to the matrimonial altar before she did, much to her chagrin.

Over the years, I watched my three older brothers leave the household one by one to university and then marriage. Father had been anxious to see his last baby bird leave the nest. With one slight push from my parents' hands, I went hurtling into society unprepared. Though I was barely able to flap my wings, they hoped an eligible bachelor of means and title would snatch me up.

My demure qualities attracted Lord Benedict Russell. We met at a weekend house party at Harold Hall. Being as equally reserved as I, it took some prodding before introductions ensued. Olivia thought him somewhat plain, but I found no aversion to his physical appearance. Tall and broad shouldered, he towered above my five-foot-four-inch frame. Although he lacked the makings of a fairy-tale prince charming, I thought him attentive, polite, and tender in his dealings with me as a woman. Those qualities in themselves produced an agreeable opinion of his character.

Did I love him? The emotion of romantic love remained foreign to me. I enjoyed his company even though he maintained a reticent personality. We had little in common regarding interests that brought us pleasure in life but were careful to exhibit mutual respect. If those qualities were the cornerstone of a happy marriage, then perhaps I did possess the emotion in spite of the fact my heart never swelled as Olivia told me it should.

The only unfavorable circumstance had been his mother, a widow, who lived with him in their stately home of Stratton Park. Her initial reaction to her son's attraction to a younger woman had been one of suspicion and distrust. Though she eventually accepted our courtship and subsequent engagement, I never sensed she wholeheartedly agreed with Benedict's choice of a wife. Admittedly, I was somewhat naïve on matters concerning the marriage bed and the running of a household. Both were tasks I found equally challenging after receiving little instruction from my mother, who doted on her sons rather than her daughter.

During our wedding night, Benedict seemingly found the experience of intercourse to be as foreign as I did. Naturally, I determined all men bedded women before they married as a rite of passage to manhood. Perhaps he had done so, but his timid approach astounded me. I didn't need to ask him to dim the lights because he did so without my plea. Neither did he beseech me to unclothe my body nor did I see the curious male appendage my mother warned me about before we wed. Instead, I crawled into bed naked beneath my nightgown and lay nervously underneath the covers.

Discreetly he reclined next to me. After a few tender kisses, he lifted my hem, positioned himself between my legs, and slipped inside my body. The swift and painful consummating encounter felt more perfunctory than passionate. He released himself and rolled off me with a groan. Our marriage, sealed in a composed regard, left a dreadful emotional chasm in my heart that grew wider over time. Afterward, my role as his wife had been a dutiful one, allowing him to bed me when he pleased. Those occasions were infrequent. Eventually I performed the task of bearing him a child.

In the sixth month of our marriage, I became pregnant. Nine months later in March of 1914, I bore Benedict his long-awaited heir to the family fortune. We named our son Percy, in honor of Benedict's father. Life between us continued amicably, and I resolved I had experienced the totality of what marriage offered. The contentment of motherhood somewhat occupied the void I felt as an unfulfilled wife.

I never doubted Benedict's love nor questioned further my endearment for him. Nevertheless, something lacked in our relationship, and as the months passed, it eventually wilted my happiness like a decaying flower. Before I could seek the answer to my growing despondency, the world around us shattered.

On August 4, 1914, England declared war on Germany. In the days that followed, the House of Commons set aside funds for an army of five hundred thousand new recruits. Benedict received his notice of mobilization among the thousands of other reserves in England.

As a major in the Royal Warwickshire Regiment, Benedict would fight against the advancing German army. Whatever solid footing I felt beforehand in our lives gave way to shifting sand as I watched my husband dress in his uniform and prepare to leave his family behind. Distraught and nervous over his departure, I feared an uncertain future. In a desperate attempt to stop him leaving, I clutched his forearm.

"You will let me come with you to the train station?"

Benedict's eyes lowered to my hand, and he gently detached it as if he were removing a piece of lint from his suit. After giving it an assuring pat, he sternly spoke. "I think it best you do not. It will be much easier, and I prefer to spare you, my darling."

His disappointing words did not deter my insistence. With equal resolve, I answered in an unyielding tone. "If you were to spare me anything, it would be not going to war." I countered foolishly, knowing it to be impossible. "I intend to spend every last second together before you depart."

He picked up his military hat and inhaled a deep breath. Tiny lines had formed around his eyes, and for the first time, I noticed the marks of maturity creep across his face. Regardless of our age difference, I believed we had many years ahead together. With a sense of urgency, I flung my arms around his neck and kissed him ardently.

The fears that boiled beneath my surface met his usual unruffled demeanor. Inwardly, I knew he disapproved of my weakness. He pulled away and thoughtfully gazed into my eyes.

"If you feel that strongly, then come with me to the station."

Thankfully, he relented, and I smiled over my successful bid to stay with him.

"Let me say goodbye to Mother first, and I'll meet you downstairs in a few minutes."

Benedict departed, and I grabbed a sweater and my purse. When I reached the foyer at the bottom of the grand staircase, Florence stood before her son. Their faces displayed little emotion, which reminded me that she, in many ways, had forged his character like her own.

"Write if you can." She calmly spoke. "And do take care of yourself."

"I will, Mother." Benedict glanced at me approaching. "Watch over Grace."

"Of course. I am keenly aware, my dear, of her needs."

After hearing her unsurprising reaffirmation of my flaws, I approached and stood by Benedict's side.

"If the military needs to commandeer the house and grounds for anything, you have my permission to do as you please," Benedict announced. "We all must do our part abroad and here at home."

"It shall be done as you wish." Florence noted my handbag and sweater. "Are you going to the station?" She flashed me a disapproving look, pressing her lips together.

"I agreed that Grace could accompany me," Benedict answered in my stead.

"Very well then."

Florence turned away from me to show her disapproval of my actions. Benedict kissed his mother on her right cheek, and we walked out the door together. As we climbed into the waiting car, a shiver of fear ran through my veins. The driver pulled slowly away from the estate as if he dreaded our destination. Benedict and I sat silently next to one another. Fearful thoughts taunted me that this could be the last time I saw my husband. When the car arrived, my eyes widened at the chaotic scene.

Hundreds of men, women, and children crowded the platforms, making it difficult to reach the railcars. Soldiers from the community had arrived to join their regiments. Already anxious over my goodbye, I suddenly found myself engulfed in a scene of tearful farewells.

Couples held each other tightly, children clung to their fathers, and tears flowed plentifully down the cheeks of concerned family members. Sucking in a breath to stifle my raw emotions, I swore for Benedict's sake not to weep.

"You shouldn't have come," Benedict said. He came to an abrupt halt and faced me. "I don't want this to be your last memory before I go."

"No, I want to be here," I assured him, grabbing his hand tightly. "I only see you and not the others. It's your face I wish to remember."

He brought the palm of his hand and cupped my cheek, looking devotedly into my eyes. "You are precious."

"Take this." Carefully I removed a picture from my purse. It had been a favorite family photograph with the three of us together. "Remember us each day and draw strength you are loved and needed." As I handed it to Benedict, an anxious frown pulled his eyebrows together. "Come home to us," I pleaded with a trembling voice.

"I'll keep it close to my heart." Benedict slipped the picture into his pocket. "Goodbye Grace."

Benedict took me in his arms, giving me a short but sweet kiss. As I clung to his body, refusing to let go, he gently pulled my arms down from around his neck until I eventually relented to his release. A moment later, he disappeared down the length of the railcars, and I saw him for one more fleeting glimpse as he turned and waved goodbye.

"All aboard!" the conductor's voice boomed. A few straggling soldiers swiftly boarded when the train whistle shrieked, announcing its imminent departure.

Women and children stood forlornly on the platforms, waving as the railcars pulled slowly from the station. Benedict had left to serve England in war, and I wondered if I would see him again.

CHAPTER 2

SHARED HEARTACHE

As noisy as it had been a few minutes ago, a somber hush filled the air. The crowd dissipated, but I stood numb, staring at the empty tracks. Off to my left, I heard a woman whimpering. When I glanced in the direction, to my surprise, I saw Olivia weeping into her hankie. We hadn't spoken since the declaration of war, but her tears told me her husband either received a call to serve or enlisted.

"Oh, Olivia," I said soothingly. My arm slipped around her shoulder. She looked up at me and blubbered.

"Have you bid farewell to Benedict too? Isn't this just dreadful?"

I shook my head in agreement, fighting back the anguish when she buried her sad face in my shoulder.

"I shall surely die if he doesn't come home. I cannot live without him."

"He will be home." I consoled her. "You must

cling to that hope and be strong, dearest, for his sake and your own." My words sounded like empty platitudes because neither of us knew what horrors the future held. Nevertheless, I loved my friend and wished to allay her fears as best I could.

Six months earlier, I had attended Olivia's wedding. She had found love with a wonderful man named Thomas Gooding, and it appeared her wish for the fairy-tale love had come true. At that time, I fleetingly pondered whether I had been too hasty in my pursuit of a husband, having missed another I should have loved instead of Benedict. All the same, I had married and committed my life to him.

"You mustn't stand here and weep," my voice encouraged. "Time to wipe your tears. Let us get a cup of tea together and talk. It's been far too long."

Olivia nodded her head and blew her nose into the hankie she had clutched in her hand. When she inhaled a shaky breath of air, I could see she had taken my advice, striving for strength instead of feebleness. With England in the throes of war, we would all need to be strong.

"Do you have a car here?" Our driver had been waiting for my return.

"No, we took a tramcar," she replied with embarrassment in her eyes.

Olivia had not married for money or status, even though her birthright could have enabled her to find a wealthy beau. Thomas did have a steady position as a tailor, but her standard of living had fallen significantly. As a close friend, I did not judge her decision to marry for love but admired her bravery.

"No matter," I replied. "My driver will take us."

We returned to my motorcar, and I gave the driver directions to our favorite tea room in Birmingham. A smile spread across Olivia's face as we pulled up to the establishment, no doubt bringing back memories of our previous outings as single ladies.

"It's been some time since we've had a cup of tea together and biscuits," I remarked. We walked into the shop, found a table in the corner, and sat down. After giving our orders, I took a moment to observe my friend. Except for the redness of her eyes from a tearful goodbye, she looked well. Her auburn hair shimmered in highlights, and her rosy complexion remained flawless. Truthfully, I missed her friendship, but since she wed, our lives had drifted apart due to her change in social status.

"I've neglected you," I admitted, feeling a prick of guilt about my lack of attentiveness to our relationship.

The server returned with our order, giving us a short reprieve from the conversation. As we filled our cups with warm tea, Olivia's friendly face soothed my anxieties.

"I've missed you too," Olivia responded. She wrapped her hands around the cup as if she were warming her fingers on the bone china.

As I studied her, I couldn't help but ask what I wanted to know. "Are you happy with Thomas?" I posed in a quiet voice. Naturally, asking such a personal question had been terribly impolite, but I hoped she would not find it offensive.

"Yes, very happy," she answered with a bashful smile. "Thomas is wonderful." Olivia studied me in return and then tilted her head. "And you?"

"Yes, I'm happy," I replied without hesitation. "Why wouldn't I be?" My voice sounded tense and defensive to my hearing. A vexed glint flashed in Olivia's eyes over my pithy reply. Aggravated about my reaction, I changed the subject from men to children.

"Percy is growing." In all honesty, he had turned out to be a somewhat chubby baby, making me wonder if he had taken on my father's weighty characteristics rather than Benedict's thin stature.

"Thomas and I have been hoping for a baby for some time with no success," she sadly announced. "We do so wish for a child, but now . . ." Her words trailed off, and her gaze lowered to the teacup.

"But now what?" I asked, not discerning her meaning. Olivia's eyes lifted to me as if I should have known her connotation.

"But now we may never have the chance if he's killed in action," she replied with a quivering lower lip.

"Oh, I see," I replied, shaking my head. "I don't know what's wrong with me. For some reason even I cannot think straight. It's all far too upsetting—war and everything. It's almost surreal."

"Don't you worry about Benedict?"

Her question caught me off guard, and it took me a minute to search my disoriented feelings that lingered after saying our goodbyes.

"Naturally, I worry about him," I replied. My brows crinkled together, which Olivia knew to be a sure sign of uncertainty in my facial expression. Good friends always have a way of discovering when you are lying about something. She reached across the table and grabbed my hand resting limply by my teacup.

"What's the matter, Grace? You don't appear happy. Now you're worrying me."

She gave my hand a good squeeze, but I pulled it away and placed it in my lap. Unsure if

I should discuss my most intimate thoughts, I slowly lifted my eyes and stared at her as the empty void within my soul reminded me of its existence. The longer I waited, the harder my heart pounded in my chest until I spoke.

"Something is not right," I admitted with despondency. "It's not that I don't think highly of Benedict because I do. He's kind to me and understanding, but when we are alone . . ." My mouth clamped shut, and I couldn't allow myself to say such things in a public setting. It wasn't proper under any circumstances. Olivia, nevertheless, would not permit me to step away from the subject.

In a whisper, she leaned toward me and asked what I dreaded. "Do you mean the marriage bed?"

As soon as the words left her lips, I felt my cheeks flush hot. My eyes pulled away, and I grabbed the last biscuit on the plate and stuffed it into my mouth.

"I take that as a yes," she said, giggling at my response. "You shouldn't be ashamed, Grace." After pausing enough time for me to swallow the treat, she continued. "If you want to talk about it further, I'm happy to tell you about my experience with Thomas." A smile spread across her face, and her eyes sparkled. I knew then she had married an ardent lover, unlike I who had married a man unskilled in the art of passion.

"Well, I should be getting back," I announced, wanting to run away from the topic altogether.

"Yes, I suppose we should," Olivia agreed. "I'm afraid I shall be dreadfully lonely without Thomas in our home." She paused and clutched her purse. "I will need to find work while he is gone because I doubt the separation allowance we receive from the military will be enough."

The idea of Olivia being unaided while her husband fought during the war chilled my soul. I didn't want her to struggle in solitary loneliness, toiling away at some meaningless job to subsidize the paltry allowance, when I, on the other hand, wandered around a grand estate with plenty of room.

"Can you not live with your parents while he's away?"

"I don't wish to inconvenience them," she commented in a cool regard. "Besides, you know they were not too happy about my matrimonial choice."

It hadn't crossed my mind the relationship with her parents remained strained. Naturally, they didn't approve of Thomas and his lack of social standing or money. Olivia, however, refused to relent and married without their blessing.

"Then come and live with me," I suggested with firm insistence. "It makes no sense to be alone." A smile spread across her face but then changed to a frown.

"But I must pay the rent on our row house. I cannot abandon our home," she stated.

It was a bit of a conundrum, but I had a fair share of funds at my disposal to assist. "Don't worry about it," I said. "Cover your furniture, lock your doors, and if it is a necessity, we can move your belongings and store them at our estate until the war has ended." It all sounded rational to me. "I'll pay your rent until we decide what to do."

"Oh, I couldn't," she protested.

In spite of Olivia's situation in life, her pride remained. "I'll hear nothing to the contrary," I spouted. "You're coming to live with me, and that is final."

"But what of Benedict's mother?"

Florence could be an obstacle that I had forgotten to consider before inviting Olivia to Stratton Park. Regardless of her objections, perhaps the time to make decisions by myself had arrived with Benedict's departure.

"I'll handle it. If Florence dislikes my decision, I shall write to Benedict and take it up with him. He is much too kind to turn you away, Olivia."

Even though I sounded confident, an ominous feeling about the future unexpectedly captured my heart. What would war do to us as a country? Would we survive and our husbands come home? Determined not to ponder on the terror of it all, I suggested otherwise.

"We will weather the storm; of this, I'm sure," I uttered with feigned confidence. "Now, let's go back to your residence, gather some of your belongings. You are coming with me."

Olivia did not object to my edict. I could tell by the beaming grin of thankfulness on her face she had found an ounce of relief from today's sorrows. We would need each other during the months ahead.

CHAPTER 3

DIGGING TRENCHES

The dowager of Stratton Park, Lady Florence Russell, had overshadowed my role as Benedict's wife since the day I wed her beloved son. My husband had been exceedingly close with his mother even after we wed, which I blamed as a contributing influence upon our lack of intimacy.

Florence had given birth to one stillborn son and suffered numerous miscarriages until Benedict came into this world. Her possessiveness was understandable, but her ability to give Benedict leeway to be his own man suffered. As a result, she ignored my opinions and suggestions, hindering my capacity to grow into the overseer of the household as I should have been. Florence refused to transfer those responsibilities in totality to me as a means of keeping control. Perhaps I could not blame her, for Stratton Park had long been her home before I entered its doors.

Benedict's father, a baron, had died nearly fifteen years prior. I believed the responsibilities that transferred to my husband upon his death had kept him from finding a wife long before we met. It was not until I married him I realized the stronghold that Florence retained upon the family estate and her son. Bringing home Olivia would be my first independent decision that I would assert upon Florence in Benedict's absence, and I knew beforehand it would not be an easy task.

After tea, I had my driver take us to Olivia's home. The neighborhood of row houses was commonplace, but personally, I would have found living in such cramped neighborhoods stifling. Our country estate outside of Birmingham, with its green landscape, trees, and abundant wildlife looked exceedingly pleasant compared to the overcrowded and dirty city that Olivia had chosen.

We entered into her residence, and though it looked spotless, the sparse furnishings saddened me. Olivia had gone from a life of riches to one of modest means for the sake of love. It was apparent Thomas possessed a quality that had given Olivia happiness regardless of his financial status.

"Do you have a housemaid?" I asked, impressed by the cleanliness.

Olivia scrunched her shoulders. "We cannot afford one."

Flabbergasted, I looked at her in awe. "Olivia, you mean to tell me that you cook and clean all on your own?" She pulled her shoulders back and lifted her chin with an air of pride.

"I do, and I'm quite good at it. Are you surprised?"

Surprised indeed, I thought to myself. "It's admirable, to say the least, after growing up in your parents' estate with servants at your every whim." Olivia had gloves on her hands, and I wondered about the state of skin from such laborious tasks. "Do you have a suitcase?" I asked.

"Yes, I do. It's upstairs in our bedroom under the bed."

"Any spare sheets?"

"A few," she answered.

"Get those for me, and I'll cover the furniture and take care of closing up the household while you pack."

Olivia glanced warily at me as if she entertained second thoughts over our arrangement and hesitated. "I don't feel right leaving everything behind," she morosely remarked.

"Well, if you don't stay with me long-term, I still think you should not be left alone today," I assured her. "Even I need the comfort of a friend nearby after saying goodbye to Benedict." I hoped giving Olivia a reason to help me would convince her to leave and allow my ploy to succeed. She stood silently pondering for a few moments and then spoke.

"All right then but just for a few days," she countered. "There's no need to cover everything as if I'll be gone for months on end—at least not yet."

She departed for her upstairs bedroom to pack while I remained behind to look around. The least I could do was check the locks on the windows and draw the curtains. While doing so, I noted their tattered settee and fading wallpaper that had curled at the corners. The wooden floor, covered with a large area rug, squeaked as I walked across it, and I wondered what else needed repair in the building. Olivia returned downstairs with a suitcase in hand.

"I think I'm ready now." She glanced forlornly at the room. "Perhaps you are right. If I stay here tonight, I shall end up crying myself to sleep."

"Then we shall comfort each other," I said, opening the door. Olivia locked it securely, and we returned to my waiting car for the drive to the manor house. My stomach knotted as I attempted to organize my thoughts on how I would approach Florence.

"Are you sure I won't be any trouble?" Olivia's voice quavered, seeking reassurance.

"Not at all." I hesitated for a moment and continued. "Say nothing to Lady Russell. Let me handle it when we arrive."

"All right, if you insist."

I glanced out the window, watching the landscape pass by the motorcar, wondering how long it would be before Benedict arrived in France to face the inevitable. In my mind, I could not comprehend what he would endure during battle. There had never been a war of this magnitude in my lifetime. Nevertheless, I wasn't so foolish as to think it an exciting endeavor to stop the Germans. Thomas and Benedict could very well die in the conflict.

The car pulled up the long road that led to the estate, and another skirmish of sorts awaited me. When we entered the foyer, Carter, our butler, greeted us.

"Do me a favor," I instructed, "and take my friend Olivia to the large guest room and help her get settled in. She will be staying with us for a few days if not longer."

Carter glanced suspiciously at Olivia and then back at me as if he were looking for an explanation to my odd request. Irritated at his hesitancy, I acted uncharacteristically by narrowing my eyes and repeating myself.

"The guest room, Carter, if you please." He appeared vexed and unlike his usual jovial self, which I attributed to the stress of Benedict's departure. A few young lads on our staff had also volunteered to fight, which would make the household short-staffed. I softened my glare, realizing he too experienced anxiety because of the changes.

"Yes, my lady," he respectfully responded. He took Olivia's suitcase and led the way up the stairs.

"Get settled, Olivia. I'll be up shortly," I instructed.

After unpinning my hat and leaving it on a side table in the foyer, along with my purse, I walked to the sitting room where I expected to find my mother-in-law. Not deviating from her usual morning routine, she sat by the window doing needlepoint. To my surprise, as she glanced up at me, the rims of Florence's eyes were red as if she had been crying. I had not expected such a reaction to Benedict's departure. Nevertheless, I had enough sense not to mention my observation that would only cause her further embarrassment.

"So how was it?" she asked.

"Emotionally draining," I responded, sitting in an armchair next to her. "The station was filled with families saying goodbye to soldiers." Realizing my comment opened a pathway to my announcement, I continued. "I chanced upon Olivia, my friend, and found her to be extremely distraught over the departure of her husband, Thomas." Florence knew little of my friendship with Olivia but acknowledged the acquaintance.

"Yes, Benedict mentioned your association with the young lady," Florence said. "Didn't she come from a respectable family but chose an undesirable match?"

When I gathered that Benedict had expressed such an opinion to his mother, I found it disturbing they had spoken on the subject.

"Despite her choice, she is happy," I countered.

Florence pulled her gaze away and returned to her needlepoint. "Well, if he's a private, he is much more likely to be killed."

My eyes closed at the tactless remark, thankful Olivia had not heard Florence's statement. Certainly, the possibility existed. Benedict, on the other hand, as gentry and from a military family, left as a commissioned major. Regardless of rank, it did not mean dangers did not exist at the front.

"Florence, I need you to keep your opinions to yourself in the next few weeks," I answered tersely. She swiftly lifted her head in my direction, no doubt surprised at the first brash comment I had ever dared to speak.

"Whatever do you mean?" Her nostrils flared.

"I have invited Olivia to stay at the estate for a few weeks if not longer. She needs to be in the presence of a good friend after finding herself without a husband for support." Trying to assert my position, I straightened my spine and pulled back my shoulders.

"Whatever for?" Florence balked, setting down her needlepoint. "Surely any support she requires should be offered by her family, not ours."

Conflict of any sort had never been my strong suit, but if I didn't continue to make known my position, Florence would soon overrule my decision.

"Her family is unable to provide provision," I stated plainly.

"You mean unwilling," Florence quipped, pulling her mouth to the side as if she already knew the reason.

Frustrated at her attitude, I persevered for Olivia's cause. "Can you not find an ounce of empathy in your heart to assist another wife who has sent her husband off to war?" Inhaling a deep breath, I pleaded to her sensibilities. "After all, we need to provide for one another and not isolate ourselves during this difficult time." Apparently, my call for decency had hit a tender spot, and I saw her hardened countenance soften.

"Quite right," she admitted with a breathy sigh. "My son did ask me before leaving to use our home as we see fit to aid in the cause."

"And Olivia is my concern at the moment, so you can see I'm sure Benedict would have no objection to opening our home for her welfare."

Rising to my feet, I smiled warmly at Florence, thankful we did not continue to argue over the matter. "I have asked Carter to take her to the large guest room in the east wing."

"You mean she's here already?"

"Yes," I replied. "Now if you'll excuse me, I need to check on her to make sure Olivia is comfortable."

Without a further word, I left the sitting room and climbed the stairs. After bravely asserting my position, my lungs expelled a few puffs of air to release the tension. When I reached the guest room where Olivia waited for my return, I smiled while I stood at the threshold, watching her look out the window. She appeared content and lost in the scenery.

"I see you are enjoying the view." Olivia swung around, her face beaming with joy.

"Truly, I have forgotten how lovely and serene the countryside can be to one's soul."

"It's the best medicine for you right now," I said, walking in and standing by her. "Why don't I get Percy, and we can take a walk in the sunshine through the gardens. Would you like that?"

"Yes, I would," Olivia enthusiastically responded.

"Good. Come with me to the nursery, and we'll let the nanny know she can have a few minutes to herself."

After preparing the pram and settling Percy comfortably inside, Olivia and I made our way outdoors. I bypassed Florence, not feeling ready to make introductions. Afternoon tea seemed a more relaxed and appropriate time.

We had settled into a leisurely stroll albeit a quiet one. Naturally, our minds focused on our husbands, and Olivia broached the subject first.

"Thomas told me he would be in training for a few weeks. Afterward, I'm not sure where they will send him. He said it could be anywhere." Her voice quavered. "What about Benedict?"

"He spoke of the front in France, although I do not believe he has received his official orders." I assumed as much because he couldn't give me a clear indication as to when he would depart. No doubt he decided the less I knew, the less I would worry, but that was not the case.

"How will they tell us?" Olivia asked, grabbing my forearm.

"You mean should something happen to them?" I carefully chose my words, not mentioning death. By the look on poor Olivia's face, I knew what she wanted to know. Olivia shook her head while biting her lower lip. "Benedict told me by telegram or letter," I answered in a somber tone. "Please let us not consider such an outcome when today they are both alive and well."

Percy started to cry, the timing of which I found distressing. We halted, and I leaned over the carriage to see why he fussed. When he saw my face, he stopped, and I smiled at him in return.

"Mommy is here, little one," I cooed. He wrapped his tiny hand around my index finger and clung to it tightly. "He probably misses his daddy."

"Is Benedict a doting father?" Olivia stood by me, smiling at Percy.

"Yes, very much so." A shade of jealousy pricked again because he did pay excessive attention to our son instead of me. Unable to hide my disappointment, I answered Olivia. "To my detriment."

"What do you mean?" She tilted her head, showing her confusion.

The door opened again, giving me an opportunity to speak my heart, but I questioned the wisdom. Olivia was my only close friend. With no one else to confide in, I relented but not without embarrassment.

"I'm saying Percy receives far more attention than I do." My eyes stayed on my son's face, avoiding contact with Olivia. The vague statement still did not reveal the totality of my disenchantment.

"Grace, I sense you wish to speak candidly with me but are holding back for modesty's sake. We are friends, are we not? Please, tell me what distresses you." Her hand reached over and grabbed mine, holding it tightly.

"Forgive me for my bluntness." I opened my mouth to speak further of my thoughts but hesitated. A blush warmed my cheeks. "Might I ask if you enjoy . . ." I could barely say the thought aloud without gulping to expel my mind. ". . .if you enjoy intimacy with your husband?" A small grin curled the corner of Olivia's lips.

"You mean sexual intimacy?"

My heart thumped in my chest when I heard the term a lady never spoke. I replied but altered her narrative to a more acceptable reference. "Well, you know, lovemaking."

Without reluctance, she continued. "Yes, Thomas and I enjoy each other's bodies very much." She giggled. "He is an ardent lover."

Ardent? I pondered the meaning of her choice of words while I pushed the carriage down the pathway. What did he do that gave her so much pleasure? Glancing at Percy, I could only conclude I had already performed my wifely duty with some expertise, having birthed a child. On the other hand, I had to admit we shared no joyous occasion underneath the bedcovers, as Benedict remained reserved and swift in his activities.

"We should not speak of personal subjects," I blurted while accelerating my step. Olivia attempted to keep up with me.

"Does he not satisfy you?"

"What?" I halted and looked at her cockeyed. "What do you mean? The act is apparently satisfying enough for men but rarely for women." I huffed in frustration.

"Oh, dear Grace," she sympathetically replied. "You have no idea what I mean, do you?"

I caught sight of a bird flying overhead, giving me the opportunity to look elsewhere and hide my humiliation. The topic had caused me distress. "Apparently not," I heard myself admit aloud. My friend was right—I had no idea what she meant.

"Benedict is much older than you," Olivia mused aloud. "Perhaps men his age are not as interested in fleshly matters."

She did have a point. Distressingly enough, I had discovered Benedict's attentiveness for intimacy had waned quite a bit a few months before the war. Naturally, I never initiated anything on my own but waited for him to advance his affections. I had to remind myself I had married a man more than twenty years my senior.

"You may be right," I conceded. Percy unknowingly decided to rescue me from the uncomfortable topic by loudly wailing. No doubt his nappy needed changing, or he needed feeding. "It appears my son has had enough of our afternoon stroll," I announced in relief. Slowly I turned the pram around and walked toward the residence.

"I assume this is the end of our discussion," Olivia stated, smirking at me like a tease.

"Well, we've come to a conclusion regarding the state of affairs, so I don't believe we need to speak of it any further. If that is the problem, then nothing can be done about it."

A shameful part of me wanted to cure my ignorance, especially my lack of satisfaction, whatever that meant. It seemed logical for me to leave the subject dormant. How could I miss something I had no idea existed? Doing my duty as a loving wife to Benedict had been all I needed to know, or so I kept telling myself. With those thoughts in mind, we returned to the house for tea and respectable conversation in Florence's presence.

CHAPTER 4

THE WORLD AT WAR

Weeks had passed since Olivia and I sent our husbands off to war. She had settled in nicely and seemed comfortable in our household. Florence continued to be cordial while Olivia was present. For the moment, we remained untouched from the conflict in Europe.

Within a month, Olivia felt anxious to return to the home she shared with Thomas, and I understood her longing to be in the midst of familiarity. She started to receive her spousal separation allowance, which would help with expenses. The city officials had set up a National War Relief Fund organized by the Prince of Wales, disbursing monies to needy families while the men were at the front. Insistent she could manage on her own, I agreed to Olivia's departure with the caveat if she needed support, she would come to me. Still concerned about her safety, I often had our driver take me for weekly visits to check on her welfare.

December arrived, and the war raged on. The opinion among the locals had been we would soon win the conflict and the men would return home. As the weeks wore on and fighting increased worldwide, I realized our patriotic notions had been prideful utterances.

The holidays came and went with little pomp at Stratton Park. We decorated the tree, attended church, and exchanged presents as required by custom but did so with little joy or fanfare in Benedict's absence. The hypocrisy of peace on earth and goodwill to men overshadowed Christmas. When the New Year arrived, we prayed 1915 would bring armistice, returning Benedict safely home.

Olivia heard nothing from Thomas until a letter came announcing unsettling news that his regiment had received their orders that he would be sailing for Egypt. The post sent poor Olivia into a tizzy.

"Egypt!" she wailed. "How could they send him so far away? It will take months to receive correspondence from him."

Once again, I had returned to consoling her troubled state of mind. Truthfully, I couldn't understand either why they sent him so far away. The war engulfed the world like a raging, untamable fire. When reading the newspapers, it looked as if every country on the face of the globe fought against another.

In the first few months, Benedict corresponded frequently. The letters arrived addressed to both his mother and myself, containing sparse details. Due to his rank, he could only convey general information, but we knew he was in France. Once at the front lines and engaged in battle, we knew his letters would be rare. I found it heartbreaking he did not write to me directly to express any personal thought or affection during our separation. Naturally, he mentioned how he missed Percy and then closed his letters wishing us well.

Spring arrived, and the community continued to rally for various causes, holding recruitment activities and numerous patriotic parades. Antialcohol campaigners from the Order of the Sons of Temperance reasserted the folly of drink as more pubs overcrowded with patrons seeking to drown their worries in ale. Temperance members expressed the evils of alcohol by pulling floats through the streets depicting two types of families. On one side, the well-cared-for wife and children by a sober head of the household. On the other side, a poor family, struggling because of the husband's overindulgence. In all honesty, I found a glass of port necessary to ease my anxieties during wartime. There were more evils in the world besides drink.

If drinking hadn't been one social concern, another rose with boys and girls coming before Police Court because of theft. Delinquent juveniles stole anything they could get their hands on in town. From pickpockets to shoplifters, the numbers increased in Birmingham as unsupervised youngsters roamed the streets while mothers worked to make ends meet. The resulting lack of childcare and no father figure to control the children exacerbated the problem.

The magistrates' answer had been to give a stern warning, but if a second offense occurred, the children received a good birching for their wrongful deeds. The newspapers reported unruly lads received up to fifty strokes with a rod! I believed the practice barbaric to beat children so cruelly, thinking they should have the minors perform restitution to their victims instead. Oddly enough, as the birching continued, the police and courts admitted to newspaper journalists the practice didn't always meet with success.

As more men left for war, new job opportunities opened up for women. The occasion gave ladies a platform to prove their abilities in spite of being the so-called weaker sex. Of course, men initially complained about females doing their work. With the majority of the male population gone, someone had to do the jobs left unattended. The situation, too, had given women an avenue to increase their voice for women's rights, which I found agreeable if nothing else.

The newspapers filled with pictures of battalions in uniform and announcements of upcoming patriotic parades as men prepared to leave for training camps. As the months passed, the sad advertisements of rolls of honor filled the columns naming the fallen in battle. There were also heroic stories of soldiers taking brave risks for king and country, who were awarded medals for their courage.

As I thought about the lonely months that could very well turn into years, I recognized Olivia and I could not stay idle or we would lose our minds with worry. As wives, we needed to keep busy. The wounded had arrived at hospitals, which were at capacity, and the representatives from the War Office and the British Red Cross Society had commandeered schoolhouses to accommodate soldiers. However, my skills as a nurse were lacking, as well as my ability to stand the sight of blood. I had no desire to help in that stead even though the need had been great.

By June of 1915, my calling had arrived. The country, now inundated by refugees from Belgium fleeing Germany's invasion, flooded the city. Olivia had been the first to show an ounce of empathy for their plight. The aldermen set up temporary housing for the influx of families, but the eventual goal was to find permanent homes during the war. A Belgian Relief Fund had been established, which aided in the expenses of their accommodations.

Olivia, in her sweetness, found a single mother with a toddler and immediately took them into her home. It filled the lonely void in her life, keeping her mind occupied with another task. With pride, I watched her give unselfishly to help another and simultaneously felt guilty I had done nothing of the sort when I possessed far better and larger accommodations to share. Benedict's mother had done nothing further regarding his parting words to use the house either. Guilty over our inaction, I felt compelled to change the situation.

After mustering enough courage to introduce the subject, I approached Florence with the suggestion we open our home to the needy. One particular afternoon, after finding her in a more than usual congenial mood, I made the proposal.

"My friend Olivia has performed a very kind and selfless gesture," I started, hoping it would open the door to the conversation.

"And what is that?" She lifted her head from the book she was reading, looking slightly miffed at my interruption.

"She has taken into her household a widowed mother and her daughter who are Belgium refugees." As I kept my gaze on her, looking for a reaction, I could not tell what she thought of my announcement. Florence said nothing, glanced down at her book, and shut it.

"I sense this introduction is about to lead us down another path," she replied. Florence folded her hands and waited for me to speak.

After shifting slightly in my seat to get comfortable, I continued. "There are many needs in the community, Florence, and I feel we have the capacity to help, but we are not."

Her lips pursed together as if she were silently pondering how to reply. Anxious to continue, I opened my mouth to speak, but she interjected her thoughts beforehand.

"Well, I suppose we could bring in a few soldiers for convalescing. Lady Beecham mentioned to me they opened their manor house to ten men."

Surprised at the suggestion, I hadn't thought she would care for the wounded to fill our rooms. Unfortunately, I hated to admit I still found an aversion to that scenario and wanted something more amenable. The mere thought of the wounded increased my anxiety regarding Benedict that he, too, could become injured or even killed.

"That may be noble, but I understand the critical need at the moment happens to be the Belgium refugees. Some of the lodgings have been taken away because of the arrival of wounded who need medical care."

Her facial expression turned sour. "You're not suggesting we fill our home with refugees? We have no idea who those foreigners are."

Her nostrils rose as if she thought it repulsive. Anticipating her objection, I already formed my response.

"There are many individuals from different classes, Florence, that need housing. I've already made some inquiries in that regard." As I watched her glare at me in defiance, I held my own, maintaining a firm but calm voice. "They are not all poor vagabonds who want to intrude upon English hospitality. Some upstanding families were displaced as well."

Florence, apparently surprised at my insistence, raised her brow. Her demeanor tempered somewhat as she inquired further.

"And do you know of any families in particular?"

"As a matter of fact, I have found two whom I think will be most agreeable to offer refuge at our home. I've already made inquiries with the Belgium Relief Council regarding their background and character."

"And who would they be?"

"A surgeon is working at the hospital. He is a widower and has a young daughter ten years of age. I understand he has a son too, but he's been wounded in battle and is recuperating locally."

"A surgeon, you say?" Florence stared at me while she continued to ponder the possibilities. "And the other family?"

"They are an elderly couple who have no other family to care for their needs. The husband is a retired schoolmaster." Purposely I lowered the tone of my voice to one of sympathy, hoping to influence her further.

"And have you met these people?"

"Not yet, but if it is agreeable to you, I will make an appointment for us to do so together. With only two families, we should be more than able to do our share, and it won't be a strain on the finances since we will receive a small stipend from the Relief Fund for their care."

To my shock, she released a puff of air noting her disapproval over my comment.

"Nonsense. The Relief Fund can keep the money and use it for other deserving families. Benedict would wish it as such for he has never shown himself to be anything but a generous man." Florence hesitated for one moment and continued. "As long as the refugees speak English—that is all I ask."

Her requirement was reasonable. Overwhelmed at her offering, I could not help myself and acted out of character. I rose to my feet, bent down, and gave her a quick hug of approval, which apparently shocked her.

"Now, now, that's enough." Florence gave me a gentle push away. "Make the appointment to meet these displaced individuals so we can work with the staff to accommodate their needs."

"Thank you, Florence." As I stood up, her eyes glistened with tears. I should not have judged her by her motives. Nevertheless, I surmised she conceded to the arrangement for her son's sake. Though she never spoke of his safety or the possibility that he might never return, like any other mother, Florence worried. She buried those fears as I had hidden mine, under the shield of good manners to show oneself strong in times of testing.

None of us had any idea if the months might stretch into years. On the other hand, constant anxiety would rob us of other fruitful endeavors while our loved ones fought the terrible war.

CHAPTER 5

WELCOME TO OUR HOMELAND

Doctor Martin Reyer and his daughter Celia were the first to arrive at Stratton Park. A few days later, Mr. and Mrs. Smit, a sweet, elderly couple who knew some English added to the assortment of boarders. Suddenly the house filled with individuals from the Continent, whose languages and culture were new to me.

The Reyers were from the southern French-speaking area of Belgium, while the Smits were from the north where the official language was Dutch. Educated and able to speak English, both Doctor Reyer and his daughter communicated well, albeit with an accent I found pleasant. Their son, Stefan, who recovered from severe injuries sustained in battle, would join us in another week to recuperate in our home. We had not the opportunity to meet him beforehand.

Florence instantly formed a rapport with Gretta. Her husband, Hugo, appeared less engaging and cautious in our midst. Surely having lost their homes and familiar surroundings had been a painful adjustment to life in England. All the same, they did their best to communicate and settle into the household.

Gretta, who was in her early seventies and spry in her step, loved to bake. She immediately immersed herself into our kitchen staff, refusing to keep idle and helping with baked goods. Our cook, Ethel, had been patient in spite of Gretta's intrusion, allowing her ample freedom to indulge the household in scrumptious pastries.

Hugo, an avid gardener, was tall and skinny as a scarecrow. He admired our beautiful landscape, insisting on helping out of doors. I held some concern they were trying to earn our hospitality but later realized they needed busy occupations to keep their minds engaged.

Doctor Reyer portrayed a somber attitude toward everyone at Stratton Park. Early in our introduction, I discovered him to be a man of few words. He possessed a full head of silver-colored hair that matched his mustache. Instead of being plump like other men his age, he had kept himself in shape and carried an air of intelligence about his personality. He routinely spent ten to twelve hours a day away from the estate, working at the hospital. With surgeons in shortage, the local health facility eagerly utilized his skills to help with the incoming wounded. Most evenings he did not take dinner with us but returned late at night and leaving at daybreak. Our driver made sure he had adequate transportation to and from the hospital at all hours of the day. It reminded me our staff had made many concessions to accommodate our new guests, and I expressed my gratefulness to each of them.

Celia, ten years of age, presented herself as a shy young lady undoubtedly affected by the uprooting from her home in the midst of turmoil. The majority of the time, her father gave her glancing kisses as he came and went, but little other interaction occurred between the two. Honestly, I felt sorry for the young girl, and being a mother myself, we swiftly bonded. After the first few days, she had attached herself to me like a lost puppy in need of reassurance and love, which I gladly gave her in return.

Her features were adorable with mounds of curly, light brown hair that cascaded down her back in an unruly mass. My first order of business was to brush through her thick locks, gather her hair together, and tie it with a large pink ribbon at the back. Celia made it clear she despised her hair because it frizzed whenever it rained. In spite of the abundance of tresses swirling around her head, she had adorable dimples in both her cheeks when she smiled.

Often I had the urge to kiss her like a doting mother but refrained from being too familiar. Florence, on the other hand, thought the girl a bit too rambunctious in her movements, noting Celia needed training on ladylike behavior.

A week later, Doctor Reyer returned home early, bringing his son Stefan for further recuperation from his injuries. Before his arrival, I had not thought much about his presence in our household. Martin had told us how fortunate he had been that his regimental officer agreed to let him oversee his care at the hospital and approve his relocation to the estate. Apparently, many Belgian soldiers arrived in England for care after a terrible battle defending their homeland.

When I first beheld him walking through the front entrance, he wore a tattered uniform and leaned heavily on a wooden cane to steady his limping gait. His tall and slender frame made him look malnourished. He bowed his head to watch his step, so I did not initially get a good look at his facial features. After halting a few feet away, he removed his military hat and glanced warily at his surroundings with a crinkled brow.

Our eyes met one another. To my surprise and without forethought, I inhaled a sharp breath. Surprised at my reaction, I pulled my gaze away and looked at his father instead. Florence arrived at my side, and for her sake, I wrestled my unexplainable manner into one of respectability. My hands folded in front of my waist stood firmly in place, but I remained unable to speak an intelligible word. Florence must have sensed my tongue-tied state of mind and swiftly turned the awkward moment around.

"You must be Stefan." She greeted him in a compassionate tone. "Welcome to our home."

"May I introduce you to Lieutenant Reyer, my son," his father responded with a proud glint in his eyes.

"Thank you for your kind . . . kind hospitality," Stefan replied with shy hesitation. He glanced at my mother and then turned his head and nodded at me. "Lady Grace, my father has mentioned to me that your husband, Major Russell, is serving in France."

His thick Belgian accent and deep voice had an uncanny soothing effect upon my ears. Poised with a direct question, I opened my mouth and spoke in a composed tone.

"Yes, that is correct. He often writes to his mother and me whenever he can, but I'm afraid his letters are less frequent than I would like." Unsure what else I should convey on the matter, I felt the need to add a positive accolade for Benedict. "We are both very proud of him."

"Well, you must be tired," remarked Florence. A concerned glance crossed her face as her eyes met his cane. "Oh dear, Lieutenant, we had planned on giving you one of the rooms on the second floor, but will you be able to navigate the staircase with your injuries?"

"I wouldn't recommend it," Doctor Reyer replied in his stead. "At least another few weeks he should not extend his wounded limb to stair climbing." He shook his head and grimaced. "I do apologize for not taking the time to speak of it beforehand. It's been so busy at the hospital that my mind completely forgot he needed other accommodations."

"Already I am a bother." Stefan sighed and shifted in his stance, grimacing as he did so. "Father is quite right; the stairs are a challenge."

Neither Florence nor I had thought about the inconvenience either. The home had no bedroom on the first floor. Even the servants' quarters downstairs were out of the question. Then an idea much more agreeable came to mind though he might think it to be a bit isolated.

"What about the cottage?" I suggested to Florence, thinking it would be a perfect location. "It's on the boundary of Stratton Park and is usually used for our hunting guests." Florence raised her eyebrow in surprise, and I feared she would balk at the idea.

"You know, Grace is correct. It's a comfortable one-story cabin. The quiet location gives a commanding view of the landscape."

"Is it far?" Doctor Reyer inquired. His brow crumpled as if he were nervous about the arrangement.

"No, not at all," I assured him in a kindly voice. "Less than a mile and we can certainly make sure that Lieutenant Reyer has everything he needs during his stay. We will send our driver to pick you up for dinner every night and bring your other meals as needed."

Feeling a bit braver, I turned my gaze back toward Stefan to assess his agreeability in the matter. "Would that be to your liking?" A cheeky but admirable smile brightened his face.

"I could use the peace and quiet," he admitted. "It's difficult to rest in a hospital." He glanced at his father. "Take no offense, Father."

"Frankly, I heartily agree recuperating in a hospital setting is far more challenging," he concurred with a wry grin.

It had been the first time I had witnessed Martin smile over anything since his arrival. As he gazed at his son, the twinkle in his eye spoke of their commendable bond. I found it difficult not to admire Stefan's physical qualities with his wavy, dark blond hair. I wondered if he and Celia had inherited their curls from their mother as one stray lock dangled on his forehead. A fair complexion accented his bright blue eyes that shimmered like the ocean waves in spite of the darkness beneath them. It was impossible not to find him physically attractive.

Perhaps I had been far too lonely with Benedict's departure, which accounted for the giddiness of heart. A desire for his companionship tempted me, confirming my need for attention. Instead of being twenty years my senior, we appeared the same age. When my thoughts indecently wandered, I checked my wild emotions with more pressing matters.

"I will speak to our butler, Carter, to have the cottage readied while we are having a leisurely dinner. They can stock some food to your liking and make sure clean linens and towels are at your disposal."

"You needn't go to too much trouble. I'm sure that I will find the accommodations comfortable."

"I do apologize it has no electric lights, but it does have running water and an indoor toilet." Rather than appearing pleased, he looked slightly distressed over the situation. "Please, as long as you are at Stratton Park, you are our guest."

"Well, come in and at least have dinner first," suggested Florence. "We already have an extra table setting."

Gretta and Hugo descended the staircase to join us for the evening meal. Not far behind them, Celia came bouncing down at full speed nearly knocking over the elderly couple to get to her brother.

"Stefan!" Her high-pitched screech echoed off the foyer walls.

"Celia!"

The two of them embraced with such enthusiasm that I giggled at their antics. Florence scowled at her exuberant entrance.

"Oh, Stefan, you are home," she cried, wrapping her arms around his waist and burying her head in his chest.

"Celia hasn't seen her brother since he left months ago," Doctor Reyer remarked. "I wouldn't let her see him in the hospital because as you know she is fond of him and the sight of his wounds would have been most upsetting."

"Oh, Stefan, I'm so glad you are back." She stepped away from him and eyed him up and down. "Papa said you were hurt." Celia scowled at the cane. "Are you almost all better now?"

"Yes, Celia, much better. The cane helps steady my walk because my leg is still regaining strength."

"Oh, what did those mean Germans do to you?" she bellowed, stomping her foot. "You should go back and kill them all."

"Celia, dinner is ready," her father interjected. "And young lady, you shouldn't say such things."

"But why, Papa? Don't you want us to win the war?"

"Of course I do, but it's not polite to wish others death."

Thankfully, the Smits interjected, steering the conversation elsewhere.

"Stefan, I presume," Hugo said. "Welcome, lad. Your father has spoken of your bravery in the field." He reached out and gave him a hearty handshake.

"Pleasure to meet you, sir." Stefan politely nodded. "And this must be your wife, Gretta. Father tells me she is talented when it comes to pastries."

Gretta grinned in return. "And I shall make whatever you like, young man. Tell me your favorite treat, and it's yours."

Stefan patted his stomach. "Not too many, I hope. I'll gain too much weight and won't be able to climb out of the trenches."

Thinking he could use to put on a few pounds, I desperately wanted to change the subject. "Let us not speak of war. It only makes me think of death," I spurted. "Dinner is ready, and we should focus on getting to know one another and building our acquaintances." Florence gave me an agreeable glance. The constant reminder of the reality around the world disheartened us both.

"I agree," Doctor Reyer added. "Let us break bread and remember the good times and speak of the peace that awaits us all."

Upon that edict, we headed toward the dining room for food, drink, and good company. Before I sat down, I approached Carter and gave him instructions to have the staff ready the cottage for Stefan with linens and towels. I wanted to make sure he had ample wood for a fire should it get chilly at night and plenty of oil lamps and candles for his use.

My eyes drifted over to Stefan, who appeared to have some trouble getting comfortable in his chair. His stiff leg made it awkward, and he kept his cane nearby. I wondered about his injury and how it happened, feeling sad he had endured the pain.

In the short few minutes I had come to be in his presence, I formed an agreeable opinion about his personality. Perhaps we would develop a friendship of sorts during his stay. Companionship with someone closer to my age would alleviate my doldrums.

At last, I sat down at the table and glanced around. The heartwarming sight filled me with deep peace. Florence and I had performed a good deed. We brought needy people into our home and used it for a worthy cause as Benedict had suggested.

CHAPTER 6

COZY COTTAGE

After dinner, I desperately wanted to accompany the lieutenant to the cottage. My eagerness to become better acquainted would take over my good senses if I didn't control the urge in Florence's presence. Instead, I asked Carter to have the driver take him and help the lieutenant get settled for a restful night. Doctor Reyer accompanied the two, no doubt to check on the accommodations. Upon his return, he joined us in the parlor, expressing his thankfulness.

"The lodgings are most delightful. It will be a quiet respite for his further recuperation." He sat down to join us for an after-dinner drink, which he had not done since his arrival.

"I'm glad to hear of it," I responded. "He is more than welcome to rest as much as needed."

"Do you anticipate that your son will have a full recovery?"

Florence's bad-mannered prying question

astonished me. My opinion had always been a person's health affairs were not for discussion like idle chitchat. Martin glanced at her with a raised brow, indicating he too thought it a bit forward.

"Eventually," he replied. His lungs expelled a worrisome sigh. "A bullet fractured his tibia during battle."

The scene played through my mind as if I were watching it like a picture show. I imagined the lieutenant running toward the enemy amidst a blast of gunfire, smoke, and death that must have surrounded him. Had he been brave or afraid?

"Another bullet entered his right shoulder, which we removed in surgery."

"Oh, dear gracious," I responded. "How was he able to get help after being wounded?" The horrified vision of Stefan face down on the battlefield sent a chill through my spine.

"A comrade-in-arms pulled him out of the line of fire." Doctor Reyer hesitated and furrowed his brow. "After the heroic deed, the soldier who saved my son had been gunned down only minutes later by a German machine gun."

Utterly disturbed, I closed my eyes to take in a deep breath.

"Such horrors." Florence groaned, her voice

trembling. "I cannot help but wonder what my dear son is enduring even as we speak."

A lump formed in my throat while asking what I feared. "If Stefan . . ." I halted in my familiarity. "Forgive me. When Lieutenant Reyer does recover, will he return to the front again?"

"He was part of the Belgian carabineers that defended Liege. If he does not regain the full use of his leg again, then I doubt he shall return."

"Perhaps that is for the best," Florence interjected. "Then your worry whether he lives or dies in the conflict will have ended."

She glanced at me with a troublesome look. Perhaps I should have agreed with her worry about Benedict but restrained my thoughts.

"Do you mind if I peruse your library and choose a few books for Stefan?" Doctor Reyer asked me directly. Thankful he had changed the subject, I readily replied.

"No, of course not. Benedict has an excellent library, and I'm sure he would want us to share."

"Very well then," he said, rising to his feet. "Would one of your staff be so kind as to take them to the cottage tomorrow?"

Without a second's hesitancy regarding thought or propriety, I volunteered. "No need. I will be more than happy to deliver the books." Pausing shortly, I glanced at Florence adding more reason behind my eager reply to assist. "As host too, I wish to make sure he has everything he needs."

"Much obliged."

Doctor Reyer took the last sip of his port when unexpectedly Florence rose to her feet and approached him. "Let me show you to the library," she said, reaching out to his forearm. "I am more familiar with its contents and can recommend books based on your son's interest."

Her shrewd move and a twinkle in her eye gave away an interest I never considered a possibility. Had she hoped to attach herself to Doctor Reyer or had Florence, like me, merely unveiled her loneliness for male companionship? My mouth parted in astonishment when they exited the parlor and strode together side by side.

Our driver brought me by motorcar to the cottage, and I instructed him to wait until I finished my call. The short visitation afforded me an opportunity to interact with the lieutenant, but I knew with sporadic interactions, forging a friendship would be difficult.

As I hugged a varied selection of books in my arms, tied together with a string, I walked to the door with anticipation in my step. Stefan's father had chosen *Moby Dick*, *The Adventures of Sherlock Holmes*, and *Journey to the Center of the Earth*. Benedict had a ferocious reading habit, and choices were plentiful while I, on the other hand, occasionally read books of poetry. The library overflowed with fiction selections from a variety of worldwide renowned authors along with the usual reference volumes and atlases. I wondered if Stefan was an avid reader even in the English language.

My fist balled, and I rapped my knuckles against the door. At first glance of my surroundings, I had forgotten about the rustic quaintness of the location. A large wooded area shaded the back of the building while the front porch gave a panoramic view of the hilly countryside. We were fortunate to have a large herd of roe deer though I didn't see any as I scanned the scenery. While inhaling a deep breath to enjoy the smell of the pine forest nearby, Stefan's voice called from behind the closed door.

"Who is it?"

"Lady Grace. I've come bringing gifts from your father and our household, Lieutenant." He didn't reply immediately, which spurred me to explain myself further. "If this is not a convenient time, I can come back later."

A few seconds later, he unlocked the door,

which I thought a bit strange that he had seen it necessary to barricade himself in for the night. I wondered if the fears of war lingered in his mind even though he was back on safe soil. When he opened it just a crack, I gave it a slight push with the palm of my hand. Stefan stood nervously fiddling with the buttons on his shirt, struggling to cover his naked upper torso. My eyes watched him close the gaping view of his bare chest. The sight caught me off guard, and I felt the heat of a blush crawl up my neck.

"Oh, excuse me," I said, swinging around and turning my back toward him. My heart burst into a frenzied beat, pounding in my chest while I waited.

After a few more seconds, he spoke. "You can turn around now." A soft chuckle left his throat. "I wasn't expecting company, I'm afraid, and have been walking around not dressed like a gentleman."

When I spun around, a cheeky smile spread across my face. Brazenly I stepped farther inside and closed the door behind me. Immediately I noticed the closed curtains, which created a gloomy interior.

"It's a sunny day," I announced. "Do you mind, Lieutenant, if I let the sunshine in?"

"No, please do. I've just kept them shut since I was in an unfit state to be seen." He glanced at my arms clutching the books and the basket of food dangling in the other. "Here, let me help you with those." Limping forward, he took them both and set them down on the table.

It had been some time since I had entered this cottage with Benedict as we rarely had cause to visit. Walking toward the window by the kitchen area, I pulled back the curtains, and a burst of light filled the interior. The front window that looked out over the porch and expansive landscape hid the scenery. With a pull of the drapery cord, it opened bringing in additional illumination.

"There, that's much better." When I turned around, Stefan stood over the books, reading the titles. "Your father chose those for you from our library. He thought they would keep you occupied during your recovery."

"He knows my interests," he nodded. "Did your husband read these?"

"Oh yes, he's quite the fan of Conan Doyle and Jules Verne. If it's not a good murder mystery, then he turns to new fiction with tall tales of other worlds," I replied, picking up *Moby Dick* and holding it. "I'm not sure what this one is all about."

"*Moby Dick*?" Stefan cocked his head at me in surprise. "Have you not read it?"

"Well, no," I quipped, feeling a bit defensive

in my response. "It's not exactly a book to keep a lady's fancy, I would think. After all, whales and seafaring stories are a far cry from Jane Austen or the works of Charlotte Brontë."

"Ah, then you do know something about it." Stefan grinned. "What do you like to read?"

"Poetry once in a while, but I'm not too keen on spending hours with my nose buried in a book, I'm afraid." Wishing to change the subject, I turned his attention to the basket. "I brought you a few pastries at the insistence of Mrs. Smit. She's been baking every day since her arrival. There are some apples, a chunk of cheese, a few hard-boiled eggs, and a fresh loaf of bread from the kitchen, compliments of our cook."

"Thank you for your thoughtfulness, Lady Grace."

"Are you finding your accommodations comfortable?" For some odd reason I walked over to the bedroom door and peeked inside the room. His bed lay in disarray with covers strewn in a pile as well as his clothes on the floor. Surprised at the mess, I offered help. "I'll have one of our maids visit daily to do housekeeping chores for you. What would be a good time to find you fully clothed?" I cast a playful glance his way and smirked.

"Probably early afternoon," he responded. "You can usually find me buttoned up by then."

After glancing around the interior once more, I took a hesitant step toward the door. "Please dine with us at the main house during the evening, Lieutenant. It is not my wish you become a hermit in these quarters but that you also become part of our family during your stay at Stratton Park."

"Of course. I look forward to the company," he replied. He flashed a broad grin. "And it's perfectly acceptable if you call me Stefan in place of Lieutenant."

Stefan leaned on his cane and took a step toward me. His nearness sent a pulsating surge of excitement through my body. "Car— The car." I stuttered. "I will have our driver pick you up at six o'clock if that is convenient."

"Yes, that will do." His blue eyes radiated thankfulness, and I inhaled a sharp breath to control what I feared my gaze displayed in return.

"Well, I shall bid you a good day." He grabbed the doorknob, opening the entry for me. My driver stood by the car, appearing a bit anxious. It suddenly dawned on me that my behavior in shutting myself behind a closed door with a total stranger might seem indecent.

"Goodbye, Lady Grace. I look forward to seeing you again this evening." His kind voice drew my attention back to him for a brief moment. When our eyes met for the last time, he grinned mischievously. "We can have a good discussion regarding *Moby Dick* after dinner."

After scowling at him in return, I responded, "Whales. What lady cares about whales?" A slight sprint entered my step as I headed for the car. "Back to the main house," I ordered, climbing inside. When I glanced at the cottage, Stefan stood in the doorway with a forlorn look of abandonment on his face. My arms tingled to offer him a comforting embrace. When the urge subsided, I exhaled a puff of air, wondering what in the world had become of my self-control.

CHAPTER 7

PHYSICAL AND EMOTIONAL PAIN

Celia stood on the threshold of the open door. Occasionally she jumped up and down in the same spot like an impatient flea. Her curls bounced wildly, straining the pink ribbon that held them in place.

"Why is it taking so long?" she grumbled. "I want to see Stefan."

Amused at her antics, I walked up beside her and noticed her hair was about to burst in every direction from the failing band.

"Soon." Shaking my head, I put my hands on her shoulders. "Stay still for just a moment, Celia. All your movement has loosened the ribbon, and it's about to fall off."

"All right." She puffed. Her face turned downward.

"Good girl." As I struggled to gather her hair again without a brush in hand, I admired the fondness Celia held for her brother. Honestly, I hadn't been that excited about my siblings growing up.

"You certainly adore your brother. Have you

always felt this way?" After pulling the ribbon tight and tying a double knot to keep it in place, she bubbled forth her answer.

"Always," she replied, smiling from ear to ear. "He's the dearest brother anyone could ever have."

"Then you are very fortunate."

"Do you have brothers, Lady Grace?"

"Oh yes, three of them as a matter of fact."

"Three!" Her eyes widened in astonishment.

"Yes, but I'm not as close to them as you appear to be with Stefan."

"Oh, that's too bad," she replied. The sound of the car arriving down the pebbled driveway perked up Celia, and she swung around. As it rolled to a stop, she ran out the door. When Stefan climbed out, she greeted him with a teasing pout of her lip.

"About time," she chided him. "What took you so long?"

Struggling to exit, Stefan leaned heavily on his cane. His facial expression appeared strained.

"Well, I cannot run here, can I?" He raised his cane and wiggled it. "My broken leg is still mending."

"Stefan, you need to get better," she admonished him in a motherly tone.

Celia wrapped her arms around him and gave him a quick hug. Afterward, she grabbed his free hand and helped him toward the door. His eyes lifted toward mine, and he grinned. Even though he pulled one side of his mouth upward, it looked as if he were more in pain than anything else. Still wearing his tattered uniform, I wondered about lending him a few items from Benedict's closet to get him a change of clothes. He needed something more comfortable.

"Are you all right?" His haggard appearance upset me.

"My leg, I'm afraid, it's been throbbing."

As he took a footstep toward me, he limped and halted.

"Well, perhaps your father can give you something for the pain."

I walked aside and let Celia help Stefan indoors. As I watched him struggle across the tiled floor toward the parlor, my stomach knotted with ill ease at his discomfort. It brought to mind the many other young men who lay in hospital beds not far away who endured greater injuries. They had lost limbs, their sight, and faces to shrapnel, while others suffered the terrible effects of mustard gas. Those dangers faced Benedict daily, and I could barely breathe at the idea of what could happen to him. I realized Stefan's presence had reminded me of the possibilities, confirming to me had we filled our house with the wounded I would have lost my mind.

"Is my father here?" Stefan had made his way to a parlor chair and quickly lowered himself down into a sitting position. He heaved a weary groan.

"Not yet. Some evenings he doesn't join us for dinner but stays at the hospital late to work." Celia sat next to her brother on the divan, continuing to hold his hand, while I took a seat across from them.

"He works far too much," Stefan replied, shifting in his seat. "He worries about me, but I worry about him employed all sorts of hours under stress."

"I miss Papa," Celia remarked. Her smile faded. "Why is he gone so much?"

"He's helping the wounded, dearest," I replied. "Many young lads need a surgeon."

"It's pleasant here compared to the hospital," Stefan added, glancing around the room. "All you can do is lie in bed, hope you don't die, while you hear grown men moan from the pain in the beds next to you." His eyes watered. "Then there are the poor lads that die regardless of treatment. I thought I had seen enough of death on the battlefield, but it followed me here to England."

As I listened intently to his comments, I became acutely aware of another type of wound the men endured. Beyond the physical pain remained the haunting horrors of war that followed them home. I didn't wish Stefan to wallow in the memories of the battlefield or the suffering and death of others. If anything, I ached to hear him laugh so I could enjoy his charming smile.

The parlor suddenly filled with the rest of the household as the Smits and Florence entered the room. Stefan attempted to stand on his feet as a matter of respect, but Hugo put his hand on his shoulder, keeping him in place.

"No need, son, to strain that leg of yours. Your respectful acknowledgment of our arrival has been noted."

"For goodness' sake, Lieutenant," Florence scolded. "Do not rise on my account either."

"You are all too kind," Stefan responded, leaning back.

"Hopefully, you find your accommodations comfortable at the cottage," Florence remarked. "If there is anything you need, just let Carter know, and he will fetch it right away."

"Yes, quite comfortable."

"Have you started to read any of the books your father chose?" I asked out of curiosity. He turned his gaze toward me and smirked.

"Ah, yes, the books. I've read *Moby Dick* before but have decided to reread it. Then I'll delve into Jules Verne and leave Holmes solving murders for last."

It dawned on me giving him books about death had not been the best of choices. "Well, if you prefer other stories, I'd be happy to take you to the library and let you look for more."

"Yes, I'd like that. Perhaps later after dinner you can show me. I am curious about your husband's collection of fiction."

Naturally, Florence interjected before I could say a word. "Yes, my son is an avid reader and collector of novels. You will discover his interests vary from the scientific to the macabre."

Stefan's brow rose over her comment, which indicated to me he would bypass the ghoulish subjects.

Carter arrived and announced dinner. Unfortunately, Martin had not yet come home. Stefan needed pain medication, and I found his absence troublesome.

"I do have some aspirin," I eagerly offered, "should you wish to take it in the interim." Without thought about my actions, I reached and touched his hand leaning on the cane. "It's troublesome to see you in pain."

Stefan glanced at my flesh resting on top of his, appearing uncomfortable with my gesture. Perhaps he thought my actions forward because I was a married woman. Pulling my hand away, I clutched in my other as we entered the dining room together. When we sat down, he responded to my inquiry.

"The offer is much appreciated, Lady Grace. If you can spare two after dinner, I will gladly swallow them to take the edge off."

"Yes, of course."

As we dined and everyone entered into conversation, Stefan, for the most part, remained quiet. Inwardly I cursed myself for touching him. In the future, I would need to restrain my eagerness.

When he finished the meal, I nodded toward Carter to fetch the medicine.

"Be a dear for me, Carter, and have one of the maids bring a bottle of aspirin for the lieutenant before we leave the table."

"Certainly, my lady."

I picked up my wineglass and sipped the remaining portion, listening to Gretta speak regarding their former lives in Belgium. She expressed her worry about her family members who were not able to escape. Purposely we had kept the newspapers for the most part unavailable. They only contained horror stories, which the journalists termed the "rape of Belgium." The reference conjured up shocking images in the public's mind. If the war hadn't been bad enough, the cruelty to other human beings sickened me.

Carter returned and handed me the medicine, which I immediately gave to Stefan.

"Take the bottle with you to the cottage," I offered.

"I don't want to take your entire bottle." He frowned as if he caused us an inconvenience.

"Do you have a headache?" Florence noted our interaction.

"No, ma'am, a leg ache." He chuckled at his answer.

"It's probably going to rain," Hugo said. "Every bone in my body aches when rain is coming, and my knees have been sore of late."

"Well, that's an interesting result of my injury. I'll now be able to predict the weather." He laughed. Stefan took the bottle, opened it, selected two pills, and then drank them down with water. When he finished, he handed it back to me. "Please, take them. I'll speak with Father when he returns."

"If you insist." Disappointed he didn't accept the offer, I retook the bottle.

"Morphine is my choice of pain medication, but Father is sparse with the drug," Stefan announced.

"It's addictive, isn't it?" Florence queried.

"It can be." Stefan fidgeted in his chair and then spoke. "That is why he refuses to give me any more."

Our dinner continued without the arrival of Doctor Reyer. Nevertheless, we all had a cordial chat around the table. After we had finished dining, Stefan spoke.

"Would it be a good time to visit the library?"

Without hesitation, I pushed back my chair and rose. "Absolutely." He struggled somewhat to rise, and Celia helped him.

"Can I come too?" she asked, looking up at him with hopeful eyes.

Stefan thought about it for a second and then turned toward me. "Do you have any children's books?"

"Oh dear, I'm afraid not," I answered. "At least not yet."

"Celia, why don't you stay with me," Florence interjected. "If you're a good girl, I might be able to persuade Carter to find you a piece of candy."

"Candy?"

The tempting offer instantly changed her focus. Stefan and I took advantage of the moment and left for the library. As we entered, he halted in the threshold wide-eyed, glancing at the walls lined with books.

"Impressive, I know," I acknowledged proudly.

"Very," he said, limping into the center. "Your husband is obviously obsessed with the written word."

Stefan's statement caused me to pause and inwardly agree Benedict was obsessed with two loves in his life—reading and Percy. It reminded me I had not been one of his passions. The thought pricked, causing my facial expression to sour. Stefan noticed my change in demeanor.

"I'm sorry if my comment offended you."

"It didn't," I replied. Not wishing to explain the reason, I walked over to one of the shelves. "He organizes the works according to the genre, so feel free to browse at your leisure."

His index finger ran across the spines of a few volumes, reading the titles. Quietly I watched his actions, admiring his hand that I had touched earlier. The breadth of his knuckles were wider than Benedict's, and his fingers were proportionate in length. I wanted to hold his hand in mine and feel the warmth of a man's touch. One thought led to another, and as my heart started to pound in my chest, I abruptly turned away.

"Well, I will leave you to search." My voice nervously quavered, revealing my discomfort. He glanced at me and frowned.

"Don't leave."

His desperate sounding entreaty halted my steps. Perhaps he felt as lonely as I did.

"If you insist, but I don't think it's wise to be alone with you in the library for any length of time." My comment had been a poor one because it suggested an impropriety between the two of us might occur.

"You have little to worry about with me, Lady Grace." He smirked. "But to ease your worries, I shall take this book, and that is all." He clutched it in his hand. "If you don't mind, I would prefer to return to the cottage. The aspirin has helped somewhat, and I want to take advantage of the reprieve and get some sleep."

"Yes, of course. I'll have Carter bring the car around." We walked to the parlor and joined the others sipping their after-dinner drinks. Celia sat on the divan, holding a box of chocolates.

"Did you find something of interest?" Florence asked.

"Yes, I think so. However, if you'll excuse me, I will be retiring for the evening."

Hugo rose to his feet. "I bid you good night, Lieutenant."

"Thank you." He glanced at Gretta and Florence. "Ladies, I bid you good night."

"Stefan, don't go," Celia whined.

"I'm sorry, little sister, but your brother needs his rest. You want me to get better don't you?" He grinned at the chocolate on her face and took his thumb to wipe where it had melted on her lips. Bringing the smeared chocolate to his mouth, he licked it off. "Hm, very good. But don't you go stuffing yourself with candy or Papa will be angry."

"Okay," she replied, giving Stefan a hug goodbye.

Obligated as the host, I accompanied him to the door. We halted, and his eyes lingered upon me as if he were studying me closer than he had in the past. For a few seconds, we silently stared at one another, and then he spoke.

"Do you miss him?"

"Who?"

"Your husband, of course."

Mortified I hadn't thought about his reference, I lowered my gaze to the floor. "Yes. Why wouldn't I?"

"Yes, why wouldn't you?" he responded, casting a wary look.

"Lieutenant, the car is waiting for you outside, sir," Carter announced.

Anxious, I opened the door for Stefan to leave, fearing he sensed my discontent.

"Good night, Lady Grace." He strode toward the car in pain as he leaned against the cane.

Unable to take my eyes off him, I watched until the motorcar had driven out of sight. When it disappeared down the road, my chest felt as if a heavy weight of sorrow had crushed it. My soul craved his companionship, and for the first time in my life, I experienced the seduction of temptation.

CHAPTER 8

FIELDS OF POPPIES

The following morning, Doctor Reyer joined us for breakfast, having on a rare occasion overslept. Dark circles underneath his eyes exposed his exhaustion, upon which Florence expressed her concern.

"Why don't you take a day off, Doctor Reyer?" she suggested. "You look utterly drained and unhealthy."

He took a sip of coffee before responding. "You have absolutely no idea, Lady Russell, of the present need for qualified medical personnel. The hospital is inundated with wounded men that need care."

"Surely one day will not hurt. Of what use will you be if you fall ill as a result of the strain?" Florence let out a puff of air showing her frustration about his stubbornness.

The conversation upset Celia, who stood up and walked over to her father. "Papa, do as the nice lady says. Don't die like Mama did and leave us all alone." Her eyes watered.

"Now, now, young lady, I'm not going to die." He pulled out his handkerchief and dabbed a worrisome tear trickling down his daughter's cheek. "Soldiers like Stefan need me to help them get well." After giving her a hug and kiss on her forehead, he nodded toward her empty chair. "Go sit down, Celia, and eat your breakfast."

"Stefan worries about you too," I said, adding to the concern. "He has expressed his distress that you are working too much."

Martin turned his head and sighed. "The children worry needlessly," he replied indifferently.

Florence and I exchanged a glance. Her miffed countenance displayed her disapproval over Doctor Reyer's attitude. Once again, I wondered if her interactions with Martin had given rise to fond feelings in his regard. As I pondered the possibility, she suddenly reprimanded him.

"Doctor Reyer, your son needs your care as well. Last night he suffered greatly with pain in his leg, and all we could do was give him two aspirins." Her cheeks flushed during her scolding discord. "Surely he is your patient as well and needs your tending."

Hugo confirmed the matter while Gretta

nodded in agreement. "Lady Russell is correct, sir. Gretta and I both noted the young man's grave discomfort last night."

Seemingly unmoved by the news, Martin dabbed his mouth with his napkin. "My son wants me to give him shots of morphine, which I refuse to do. It will only lead to addiction." He rose from the table and glanced at everyone as if this were his last word on the subject. "Aspirin is sufficient. The lad needs to brave through the discomfort."

The cold and seemingly uncaring remark angered me. When I opened my mouth to give him a piece of my mind, I suddenly clamped it shut when Florence caught my eye, shaking her head negatively.

"If you will excuse me, I have work to do." Martin threw his napkin down on the table.

Poor Celia's eyes grew wide as her father stormed from the dining room, leaving all in attendance flabbergasted. If it weren't for Celia sitting at the table with us, I would have raised my voice to complain of his unsympathetic regard toward his son.

"What a shame," Gretta said in a low voice. "I'll have to bake the young lad a good apple strudel today."

"It's none of our business," Florence responded. "Stefan is his son, and as his surgeon and father, I'm sure he has his best interest at heart."

"Well, we better have Carter purchase additional aspirin from the chemist," I announced. "It's only fair the lieutenant have some relief for his aching leg."

"Yes, I think that would be wise," Florence readily agreed. "But let us not tell Doctor Reyer lest we offend him by interfering."

After breakfast, I went to the kitchen to have the cook prepare another basket. We filled it with boiled eggs, cheese, and freshly baked bread. I added a jar of strawberry preserves as a sweet treat. As I thought about what else I might bring Stefan, it suddenly dawned on me an occasional shot of whiskey wouldn't do any harm to take off the edge. Since Benedict had an ample personal supply for his enjoyment, I doubted he would miss one of his unopened bottles.

"Shall I call the car around?" Carter offered.

I didn't want to be accountable for how much time I spent at the cottage and decided to forgo the transportation. The morning sun radiated across the landscape, and with a basket in hand, a twenty-minute walk would do me good.

"No, I think that I'll walk, Carter. It's far too nice of a day, and I wish to take advantage of the sunshine."

"Very well, my lady," he responded. Carter

thankfully hadn't thought any less of me for daring to visit the lieutenant alone. After all, as far as he knew, I was merely delivering food and a bottle of aspirin. Naturally, I mentioned nothing about the whiskey I hid in the bottom of the wicker basket.

After a few minutes, the walk had an invigorating influence upon my mind. A winding dirt road led to the cottage, which had a slight uphill slant. Puffy white clouds traveled overhead pushed along by a warm breeze. Wild field poppies dotted the landscape as they started to bloom. They waved back and forth, dancing to the wind. It created such a beautiful scene that I halted for a few moments to enjoy the interspersing of green and red hues. As I surveyed the flowers, I thought of Benedict. He would benefit from the beauty.

While gazing at the brilliant crimson flowers, the realism of the world at war disturbed my peaceful thoughts. The pleasant moment gave way to a terrible sense of woe as I thought about the men dying around the world. Abruptly, the flowers nestled among the greenery transformed into droplets of blood scattered across the field. Clusters of poppies, growing tightly together, became red pools of crimson swaying in the air current. The vision clutched my heart with horror. Instead of lingering to observe the sight any longer, I sprinted toward the cabin to escape the unbearable change in scenery, reminding me of blood and death.

Out of breath and trembling from the eerie portrait of destruction my mind had painted, I knock loudly on the door. Stefan did not answer immediately, but when he did, I pushed my way indoors and slammed it behind me. My back leaned against the frame, struggling to hold back tears.

"For heaven's sake, Lady Grace, what in the world is the matter?"

"Poppies," I murmured, thinking it ludicrous I had become so upset at a field of flowers.

"Yes, I've noticed they have begun to bloom. Quite pretty actually."

My eyelids remained shut, trying to erase the visualization.

"Do you not like them?"

"I used to," I replied, opening my eyes. "As I stood there looking at them, the field turned into blood, reminding me of the war."

"Oh, I see." Stefan's facial expression saddened. He took the basket from my trembling hand. "Come and sit down."

Without hesitation, I took a chair. Stefan stared at me for some time, no doubt considering my vulnerabilities. Embarrassed, I inhaled a deep breath. "Much better now," I announced.

"Forgive me. I have an overactive imagination."

"Nothing to forgive," he replied, taking a seat across from me. "When it rains, all I can see is the mud of the battlefield that I wallowed in for days on end."

Having arrived at a moment of composure, I looked at Stefan. Dressed casually, with a buttoned shirt this time, he appeared relaxed. A good night's sleep had seemingly helped to restore his health.

"You look rested."

"Yes, I am, in fact. Thanks to the aspirin last night. And thank you for a comfortable change of clothing."

"You are more than welcome. Walking around in a scratchy wool uniform must have brought you discomfort." After inhaling a breath of air and embracing the calmness of emotions that had returned, I rose to my feet and walked over to the table where he had set down the basket.

"I have some things for you."

"Fresh bread, no doubt. I can smell it." He stood next to me. "Thank the cook, will you?"

"Yes, there are boiled eggs, cheese, bread, and preserves."

"You're spoiling me." He grinned.

"Let me spoil you some more." I pulled out the bottle of whiskey from Benedict's supply of liquor.

"Good heavens!" he bellowed. "Whiskey?" Stefan grabbed the bottle and read the label. His eyes sparkled. "If you weren't married, I would kiss you for this generous gift." He snickered, clutching the alcohol as if he had found water in a desert.

Please do, my thoughts replied, but my mouth remained shut. "I'm sure Benedict wouldn't mind my sharing it with you." For some odd reason I had to bring my husband into the conversation to control the circumstances. "Oh, and this too." My hand reached into my pocket and pulled out the bottle of aspirin. "Here, take this and keep it. Carter is getting more from the chemist today." Stefan took it in hand.

"Thank you for the generous gifts, Lady Grace." He set the bottle of whiskey down on the table along with the aspirin. "I can't remember the last time I've had a decent drink."

"We mentioned your discomfort to your father this morning at breakfast. I had thought he would supply you with something stronger for the pain but refused."

"I'm not surprised," Stefan said. He limped over to the chair and sat down. "He uses other drugs sparingly not wishing me to become dependent."

"That may be understandable, but I despair

seeing you in such discomfort, Lieutenant."

"Stefan. Please call me Stefan."

"All right, Stefan," I replied. Saying his name felt delightful on the tip of my tongue.

"If it's any consolation, you've made me a happy man this morning." He nodded at the bottle. "Best not tell Father about the spirits. He would disapprove as he is actively involved in the temperance movement."

"I wouldn't think of it." I assured him with a grin.

We smiled warmly at each other for a few seconds, and I wondered what he thought of me as a woman. Did he think me attractive? As I pondered the unknown thoughts in his mind, he suddenly changed the subject, drowning my imaginings.

"Have you heard from your husband recently?"

My husband. One minute I cringe at the thought of him dying in a pool of blood like the fields of poppies, and the other I push him out of my mind as if he were nonexistent. When in Stefan's presence, he does not fill my thoughts. The lieutenant, however, appeared intent on returning them to where they should be, probably sensing my weakness.

"The last letter we received arrived about three weeks ago from France." The smile on my face faded as I struggled with the irritation the question produced.

"Well, I am sure that he is fine," Stefan replied. "I'm curious though, you said *we* received. Does he not write to you and his mother in separate correspondence?"

Surprised he had noticed the combined means of communication, I answered bluntly, "No, the letters are addressed to the two of us."

"Then he expresses no personal thoughts to you separately?" His eyes narrowed at me in curiosity.

"Such as?"

Stefan didn't respond directly. Instead, his gaze softened as he surveyed me sitting in the chair next to him.

"Such as how much he loves and misses you," he calmly remarked.

It took me a moment to gather my thoughts so I fiddled with a wrinkle in my dress to bide time. "My husband, Lieutenant," I slowly began, "is a man of few words and even fewer when it comes to expressing any personal views in that regard." My voice sounded terse, confirming my frustration. He shifted uncomfortably in my response and pulled his eyes away from me. Oddly, I felt the need to return to addressing him by rank.

"I'm being rude and prying into matters that

are none of my business. My apologies, Lady Grace."

His demeanor toward me changed as if he, too, realized he needed to rein in our private meeting and keep our sentiments to a minimum. I held captive my thoughts about my marriage far too long except for the moments I fleetingly expressed my unhappiness to Olivia. Having another opportunity to do so, I desperately wanted to declare my sorrow for the attention, passion, and intimacy I failed to receive from Benedict. Unable to stop myself from the emotional drought in which I found myself, words gushed from my mouth as if floodwaters had broken down the cottage door.

"My husband is twenty years my senior. When I married him, our age difference did not concern me. In fact, I gave no thought whatsoever what my life would be like at Stratton Park married to a baron." Inhaling a breath to curb my threatening tears, I continued. "I'm sure that he loves me, but his ability to express such emotions is lacking. He is a man of restrained passion, you see, except for his books and son."

When I realized my body trembled as I sat in the chair, I jumped to my feet. My mouth had spewed my marital deficiency to a complete stranger when I should have gagged myself from doing so.

Stefan sat quietly, watching me with regard, then rose to his feet. His hand touched the side of my warm cheek with his fingertips. When he did so, I flinched and grabbed his wrist to prevent him from stroking me further.

"Please don't," I whispered. Emotionally weak and confused, I admitted if I allowed Stefan to continue, I would not want him to stop. He relented and dropped his hand to his side.

"I find it disturbing your husband has neglected you emotionally. If you were my wife . . ." He halted his words. His blue eyes grew a shade darker.

He had not finished his sentence, which I found unacceptable. I needed to hear his words. "If I were your wife, what would you do?"

Stefan studied me, gazing at my form standing before him. He expressed a heated desire through a mere glance. He didn't need to answer my question verbally because he had succeeded in exposing his meaning otherwise. Remembering my conversation with Olivia, I realized Stefan Reyer had the power to give me the missing piece in my life. In a strained tone, he spoke.

"You should go." He stepped around me and opened the door. "Thank you again for the food, drink, and aspirin. I appreciate your thought-fulness, Lady Grace." His tense words exposed a struggle.

My eyes averted his to keep myself from relenting to temptation. "You are welcome, Lieutenant."

A second later, I sprinted down the path toward the manor house as if I were fleeing the fires of hell itself. The red poppies filled my peripheral vision, but I refused to glance to my right or left. Stefan, my husband, and red flowers all threatened to ruin what I thought would be a beautiful day. Instead, they reminded me of death on one hand and unfulfilled passion on the other. To my utter shame, my body ached with need, and I knew my face had turned as crimson red as the flowers in the field.

CHAPTER 9

DOLLS AND KITES

The following day, I wandered around the manor house with a troubled heart. Little conversation had ensued with the lieutenant at yesterday's evening meal. I was too embarrassed to look at him in the eye and kept my attention on the Smits and Doctor Reyer, who had joined us.

The entire morning, Celia had demanded my attention, which I half-heartedly gave. She wanted to play dolls, and when she handed me the one she owned, I didn't want to touch it.

"Is that the only doll that you have?"

She grinned as if it were the most prized possession in the world. "Mama gave me this doll," she remarked with sad eyes. Celia held it up in front of my face. Its legs lifelessly dangled with one shoe missing. A dirty and tattered pink dress clothed the toy. "I named her Marie just like Mama's name."

The doll had a beautiful face, but its body was in need of good cleaning and repair.

"Why don't we take the dress off Marie and

give it a good wash and mending. The sleeve is torn."

She looked at the doll and hugged it closely to her chest. "I don't know if I want to let her go." She pouted.

"You want her to look pretty, don't you?"

"I suppose."

"I promise to take good care of her, Celia. You can trust me." When I held out my hand, waiting for her to give me the doll, she stared at it for a few moments. "We'll mend her dress, wash her face, and she'll be brand new." I enticed her further.

"Okay," she relented, shoving the doll in my direction.

Gently I held it up and smiled at the raggedy plaything. "Hello, Marie. I promise to take good care of you."

"When can I have her back?"

"In a day or two," I replied. Naturally, I would have to consult the housekeeper about the task ahead but knew she would do a good job of restoring it for Celia.

"Well, what am I to do in the meantime?" She crossed her arms over her chest. "I'm bored."

"So I see." Her juvenile antics reminded me of myself when I was ten. "Well, what else would you like to do?"

"I don't know," she grumbled.

"Take a walk?"

Her eyes brightened at my suggestion. "Can we go see Stefan?"

"Stefan?" I balked. "Whatever for?"

"He can make me a kite to fly," she spewed with exuberance. "He's really good at kite making."

"Dearest, I don't think he has anything to make a kite with, I'm afraid. There is nothing at the cottage." Truthfully, I wasn't too keen on seeing him, especially after yesterday.

"Oh, please," she whined. "Please, please, please."

She grabbed my hand and squeezed it tightly, and I knew if I didn't relent, Celia would never forgive me.

"All right, if you insist." I surrendered. "I'll get Carter to bring around the car."

"Thank you." She squealed, throwing her arms around my neck. I had to admit that her exuberance had become contagious. In spite of the embarrassing moments that transpired between Stefan and me the other morning, I would enjoy seeing him again. With Celia in the midst, surely it would control any dangerous urges I might entertain.

"Give me a few minutes to talk to the butler, and we'll leave." Celia grinned at me and started to jump up and down, which I had learned was her favorite way of releasing energy.

I found Carter in his small office in the servant's quarters and gave him a laundry list of things to do.

"Is there something you need?" he asked, rising to his feet. Carter looked a bit surprised I entered his domain, which I rarely did.

"Yes, a few things, actually. First give this doll to the housekeeper, have her wash and repair the dress. Also, the body and face need a good cleaning."

"For Miss Celia, I take it." He regarded the old toy with a raised brow.

"Yes, it's very dear to her, so please take good care. It was a gift from her mother." I held it out for Carter to take in hand. When he did so, he grimaced, holding it an arm's length away from his body. I could barely contain my laughter.

"Anything else, my lady?"

"I'll need the car to take Celia and me to the cottage." I was about to leave, but then it dawned on me we might have the makings of a kite here at the manor house. "Oh, Carter, what are kites made of?"

"Kites?" He cocked his head over my surprising question.

"Yes, kites. Celia wishes the lieutenant make her a kite to fly, but I have no idea if the cottage provides the necessary components for such a flying thing."

"Kite flying." He grinned. "Was one of my favorite pastimes as a boy."

"Really?"

"If you will give me fifteen minutes, I might be able to give you the items needed for the lieutenant to use for this outdoor endeavor."

"You're a lifesaver, Carter."

"Always at your service, my lady," he replied with a proud glint in his eye.

A half hour later, Celia and I met Carter in the foyer, carrying a bag of items. "For the lieutenant's use." With a confident grin, he named the contents. "Newspaper for the body of the kite, glue, a pair of scissors, a ball of string, and a small strip of lightweight cotton for the tail." In his hand, he held two thin sticks—one long and one shorter. "Freshly cut from the birch tree in the garden." He lowered his voice. "Please, not a word to the gardener or he'll have my hide."

"You are a dear, Carter," I said. "Well done."

"I'm so excited!" Celia squealed.

Florence, having heard the entire ruckus, entered the foyer and approached the three of us with a scowl. "What is going on here?"

Carter looked mortified as if he were in for a vigorous reprimand.

"We are going to visit Celia's brother so he can build a kite for her," I calmly announced.

"Carter has provided everything we need."

"Do you think it is wise to be bothering him with such frivolous activities when he needs his rest?"

Her attitude irked me. "I spoke with him yesterday morning, and he appeared far more relaxed and pain free. Didn't you notice it last night at dinner?"

"Yesterday morning? What were you doing there by yourself?"

"I delivered the bottle of aspirin, bread, eggs, and cheese, and then promptly left." My nerves tingled as I defended my actions to my mother-in-law. I knew she would think it improper.

"Well, I don't see the need for you to be traipsing there on your own when Carter here is very capable of taking anything needed to the lieutenant."

Her terse tone scolded me in front of the staff and Celia, which I found embarrassing. Supposedly, I deserved the rebuke since I was a married woman. Unable to defend my inappropriate action further, she looked at Carter and barked her order.

"Carter, if the lieutenant needs anything, you should see to it yourself or one of the other staff. Is that understood?"

"Understood, Lady Russell," he swiftly replied, avoiding eye contact with me.

"Does this mean we can't go see Stefan?" Celia asked with tears welling in her eyes.

"It certainly does not," I replied, giving Florence an angry glare. "Celia and I will be visiting so she might have time with her brother. We will all return well before dinner."

Florence glanced at Celia, who stood sadly before her with puppy dog eyes and a heart about to break into a million pieces. She shot a wary glance at me, holding the bag of kite-making bits and pieces.

"Be back at least an hour before dinner is served," Florence firmly instructed.

"Of course," I answered demurely, keeping my anger in check. With my free hand, I took Celia's and led her outdoors for her afternoon adventure.

CHAPTER 10

LAUGHTER IS THE BEST MEDICINE

With a bag of construction materials, Celia and I arrived at the cottage. Eager to see Stefan, she ran to the door and knocked, adding her voice to announce our arrival.

"Stefan, it's me, Celia!"

It didn't take long for him to swing the door open. He looked surprised at our arrival, standing in the doorway in his pants, with a white undershirt and suspenders. Once again, he hadn't entirely dressed.

"I thought you said you'd be fully clothed by this time of the day." I eyed him up and down.

"Well, I was, but after the maid left making my bed and straightening up my messes, I took my shirt off." He smiled at Celia. "What are you doing here?"

"You must make a kite for me, Stefan," Celia demanded, pushing past him into the interior.

"A kite? But—"

"No buts, Lieutenant. We have all the makings here in the bag, plus two birches for the frame." I shoved the bag in his direction.

"So I see. Well, you might as well come in while I start my assigned task."

Stefan stepped aside as I entered and then closed the door behind me. He glanced at me with a warm smile, and I returned the sentiment happy to see him again. Celia interrupted the two of us.

"Well, stop dilly-dallying, Stefan. We only have a couple of hours to fly it before dinner." She thrust her hands on her hips.

"All right then, let me see what components you have brought to do the job."

His hand delved into the bag and pulled out the rolled newspaper, glue, string, and pair of scissors. After examining the frame material, he approved.

"These are super."

"Chosen by Carter," I added. "Apparently, he is a kite expert too."

"All right then. Celia, are you helping? Choose two pages from the newspaper you'd like to use, and I'll start building the frame."

I stood and watched with amusement as Stefan acted as the surgeon and Celia as the nurse, handing him the implements to make their flying paper with strings. The process looked curiously complicated with the sizing of the object, cutting the form, gluing it together, and adding a tail. The two had obviously done this before. The sight of brother and sister working together warmed my heart. After nearly thirty minutes of intense effort, the kite was ready.

"You're lucky there's a strong breeze outdoors, Celia. Let's go and try it out," Stefan said. He flung open the door and limped outdoors, using his cane for support. "Now, sweetheart, you're going to have to do all the running to get this up in the sky. I can't help you this time because of my leg."

"Perhaps I can help," I offered.

"I can do it by myself," she adamantly declared.

"Remember what I told you, Celia. Run as fast as you can and let the string out bit by bit. When the wind catches it, make sure you hold on tight."

Not waiting for further instructions from her brother, Celia ran down the dirt road. On her first attempt, she almost caught the wind, but the kite took a nosedive into the dirt. Undeterred, she picked it up and started again.

"That's it, Celia!" Stefan yelled. "You've got it now."

She did. The kite ascended, and Celia halted her step, giving it more string. The tail wiggled back and forth as if it were waving at her in delight.

"She's very good at it, isn't she?" Celia handled the task astonishing well.

"It was our favorite activity back home," Stefan replied.

After he had made the remark, I noticed the smile fade from his face. Lines of sorrow crinkled his brow. As much as I empathized with his family's loss of home and country, I could not comprehend the pain they must have felt.

"Tell me about your home in Belgium, if it's not too painful to talk about it." Stefan's eyes remained upon Celia, but I noticed his jaw tensed. He did not answer me straight away but kept watching his sister's carefree playtime.

"There is not too much to tell," he announced in a strained tone. "We lived in Luxembourg. Luckily, Father had the sense to escape with Celia before the city came under siege."

"I'm so sorry, Stefan. I can't imagine how horrible and frightening it must have been for them." I paused as his painful countenance remained. "And for you, fighting at the front to save your country."

"Well, we've lost our country, but hopefully the war will be won."

"Yes, of course," I agreed with enthusiasm. "And then you can return home."

"Yes, though I often wonder if I will have anything to go back to."

He turned his head and glanced at me for a few seconds. Suddenly I wondered if he had left behind someone he loved. It was foolish of me not to think he loved another woman. Nevertheless, I could not ask him such a prying question to satisfy my curiosity. The moment, at least for me, had become strangely awkward, and I put my attention upon Celia. To my delight, she continued to enjoy the kite until a strong gust of wind violently hit the paper. The strain upon the newspaper caused it to rip, sending it spiraling to the earth.

"Stefan!"

She screamed for her brother. He leaned on his cane and limped in her direction. Unable to come to her rescue as quickly as she would have liked, Celia stood in the dirt road scowling at the broken kite. When he came to her side, she stomped her feet.

"It broke," she snarled. "Darn wind!"

I glanced off to the left and saw it had landed among the poppies and headed in its direction. A few moments later, I recovered the broken masterpiece and brought it back to its creators.

"Well, I don't think it can be fixed," I said, handing it to Stefan.

"Yep, ripped the paper." He scrutinized it.

"I'm afraid we'll need more materials to fix it, Celia."

"Oh, that's okay." A slight pout pushed out her lower lip. "I had fun while it lasted."

He put his hand on her shoulder. "You're a good sport."

"Maybe we can do it another time?" Her eyes lit up at the thought.

"Yes, that's fine with me. Next breezy day come up to the cottage, and we'll try it again."

Celia tugged on my arm.

"Can we go home now? My tummy is growling."

Her change from anger to hunger amused me, reminding me how flexible and changeable children can be. A part of me wished I could return to those happy and carefree days of childhood.

"Yes. It's time for an afternoon snack before dinner," I said.

"Don't go." Stefan interrupted. "I have some cheese and bread in the cottage. Why don't you both come in and have a bite to eat?"

"I better not," I swiftly replied. The anticipation of Florence's disapproval hindered my acceptance. "Celia, if you'd like to stay here with your brother, I'll have the car come get you both for dinner. Would you like that?"

"Oh, yes." She gripped Stefan's hand. "You

don't mind, do you?"

"No, of course not. Run along inside while I say goodbye to Lady Grace."

"Okay."

Celia did not hesitate to sprint back to the cottage, leaving us alone for a few moments. In truth, I didn't want to leave. Being in Stefan's presence exhilarated me.

"Thank you for bringing her here to fly a kite. That was thoughtful of you."

"Well, it was her idea." I dismissed the notion that I held any responsibility. "To be honest, I enjoyed watching the two of you together. She's an extraordinary girl."

Unexpectedly, he tenderly took my hand in his and held it. "Your hospitality to our family has allowed us to heal in more ways than one."

When he touched me, a warmth of adoration filled my entire body. My eyes lowered to his lips that I yearned to taste for hours on end. Moreover, an extraordinary urge to embrace him caused me to tremble. Afraid I would act upon the scandalous desires, I tugged my hand away from his and held it in my other.

"I should go," I said, stepping back. "Florence will wonder why I'm not tending to Percy this afternoon." Indeed, she would wonder, because I had neglected my son today to enjoy the company of another man who was not his father.

Stefan shoved his free hand in his pockets as if he needed to keep it in check. "Well then, I'll see you later for dinner."

"Yes, dinner." After smiling softly, I turned and walked down the road to the manor house. My feet felt as if they were walking on clouds while continuing to enjoy the sensation of his hand in mine.

Upon my return, I saw Florence gazing out the parlor window. By the sour look on her face, she had been looking for my return. As soon as she saw my approach, the curtain fell back into place. A rush of embarrassment over the inappropriate sentiments my heart entertained caused my stomach to knot. With Florence's uncanny ability to see right through me, I attempted to rein in every emotion that would expose my feelings to my mother-in-law. When I entered the door, she stood in the foyer, waiting for me like a predator.

"Where's Celia?"

At least she didn't accost me straightaway about spending time with Stefan. "She wanted to stay with her brother until dinner, so I agreed." Not wishing to remain any longer, I stepped past Florence to head upstairs, thinking I had skirted the brunt of her displeasure. In my haste to leave, she gripped my forearm, halting me in my place. Her fingers harshly clutched my flesh.

"You are spending too much time with that young man, and I don't like it." She huffed. Her eyes narrowed into accusatory slits. "Your husband is putting his life on the line at the front while you run off and fly kites with a stranger."

"It was a simple activity to give Celia a moment of joy. In fact, it was the first time I had seen the lieutenant laugh since he arrived."

"Nevertheless, it's inappropriate," she sternly reiterated.

"Laughter, they say, is good medicine for the injured. Bringing the refugees here to our home is more than giving them shelter, Florence. It's our duty to help heal their souls as well."

Surprised at my self-righteous rant, I admitted those had not been my motives at the onset. Nevertheless, having only a few minutes ago witnessed Stefan's sorrow over the loss of their home in Luxembourg, the extent of their pain became evident to me.

"Regardless." She huffed in exasperation. "I forbid you to go to the cottage alone."

Forbid? Her edict angered me. "Obviously, you do not trust my devotion to your son," I declared indignantly. "I'm merely being a good Christian by showing our hospitality and making sure his needs are met."

Florence dropped her hand from my arm. In swift retreat, I sprinted up the staircase to my room and slammed the door behind me in anger. Without a doubt, I knew her to be right. Any further time alone with Stefan would only encourage my affections while the thoughts of my husband faded into obscurity. It frightened me, but I felt helplessly drawn to the young man who declared, "If you were my wife . . ." When he spoke those words, I wondered if he possessed the power to fill the void in my soul.

CHAPTER II

A FRIEND IN NEED

After a few weeks had passed, I awoke with the urge to flee the manor house and get away. My muddled emotions and my weak will ached to see Stefan every waking moment. The brief dinner hours were not enough to satiate my hunger for his companionship. To appease Florence, I refrained from visiting the cottage. After dinner, we spent brief interludes of frivolous private conversations, albeit under the watchful eyes of everyone in the household. There were days I felt stifled and unable to take a deep breath.

After informing Florence I would be going into town to see Olivia, she gave no objection. I had neglected my friend for some time. With the Reyers and the Smits in our midst, I had focused on nothing else except my selfish pursuits and their needs.

When I arrived at her home, my first inclination upon seeing a friendly face had been to throw my arms around her neck. I didn't prevent myself from doing so either and hugged her tightly.

"Oh, I've missed you," I moaned. She deserved my apologies for hours on end. Over her shoulder, I saw her Belgium ward, Anna, and her little girl. After crushing Olivia in an embrace, I took a step in their direction. "Hello."

"Good to see you again, Lady Grace," she responded, holding her shy daughter's hand.

"You know, I have a little girl named Celia staying at my house. She is ten years old. Perhaps the two of you should meet, and then you can play dolls together. Would you like that?"

A large, agreeable grin spread across her face, and her eyes lit up.

"Indeed, she would enjoy it very much," Anna replied. "Playing with another child from her homeland would certainly be a treat."

"Well then, we will have to arrange it very soon." I turned my attention to Olivia. "Have you heard from Thomas?" After hearing my question, her eyes dulled and she shook her head.

"No, not as often now that he is in Egypt. In his last letter I received weeks ago, he stated that he would be traveling to Turkey."

"Turkey?" My voice squawked at the surprising announcement. "Is he in Gallipoli?"

Olivia shrugged her shoulders. "I don't know. What is Gallipoli?"

Her answer told me she had not been reading the newspapers and perhaps just as well. The latest British and French offensive in Gallipoli were reporting heavy losses. Naturally, I worried about instilling fear into Olivia unnecessarily and decided to point her attention elsewhere.

"It's just a place in Turkey, that is all," I replied, shrugging off her question. "Now, let's not speak of war. Why don't we all go out for lunch together? My treat."

"You should go and spend time with your friend alone," Anna suggested. "My daughter and I had planned to take a walk together."

"Are you sure you won't come?" Olivia said.

"Yes, very sure."

"Well, all right, if you insist," she replied. "Let me fetch my hat and purse." Olivia ran up the stairs, leaving me alone with Anna.

"You are very kind to let us have a few moments alone," I replied, realizing she offered us the time together.

"She has missed you, and Anna and I did plan on taking a walk in the park. I don't wish to disappoint her."

Olivia bounced down the stairs. "Ready."

We left and strode down the street to a little café on the corner. "How is Benedict? Have you heard from him?"

"Occasionally he writes to us," I answered

nonchalantly.

"Us?"

"Yes, he writes to Florence and me in the same correspondence."

"You mean his mother and you?"

The painful reminder made it difficult to inhale a deep breath. I didn't answer because we had arrived at our destination. After sitting down, I pulled off my gloves and picked up the menu, avoiding eye contact with Olivia and embarrassed over my husband's lack of intimacy. Instead of discerning the awkwardness of her question, she continued the exchange.

"I gather, then, Benedict does not write to you personally," she stated.

My eyes met her empathetic glance. "You have assessed the situation correctly. He writes of the war and his efforts but glances over private thoughts and expresses platitudes of how much he misses us." I emphasized the plural form. Irritated over Benedict's coldness, I spat my mind. "Besides, the man knows nothing about how to be intimate, even on paper. I'm not surprised by his actions one bit."

"Oh dear," Olivia replied. She leaned back in her chair and gawked at me in surprise.

The waitress came to our table, and we gave our orders for tea and sandwiches. The exasperation regarding my husband's actions lingered, tainting the closeness I had wanted with Olivia. There were other matters of greater concern I wished to confide in, and I fiddled with the napkin, attempting to decide whether it wise to do so.

"How are your boarders?" Olivia asked.

"They are congenial." A smile had replaced my frown as I thought of Stefan.

"The Smits are a sweet couple. Gretta is constantly baking in the kitchen, while Hugo tends to the garden. They have kept themselves busy in the household, which I think is good for them."

Our tea arrived, and I turned my attention to adding a spot of milk and sugar. Olivia continued questioning the arrangement.

"And the surgeon, is he often there too?"

"No, I'm afraid he spends long hours at the hospital. He rarely dines with us in the evening." After taking a sip of tea, I continued. "However, Celia is an enjoyment. I do think it would be wonderful to have the girls get together in the near future."

"Yes, that would be delightful."

"And Lady Russell, does she get along with everyone in the household?"

"Yes, well. She finds Doctor Reyer's conversations stimulating." A smirk curled my lips. "In fact, I sense she is interested in developing a relationship."

Olivia laughed. "Oh dear!"

"Yes, it's quite amusing."

Olivia thoughtfully sipped her tea while I mustered the courage to speak of Stefan.

"A few weeks ago, Lieutenant Reyer joined us. He had been discharged from the hospital but is still recovering from a severe leg wound."

"You mean Doctor Reyer's son?" Olivia's eyes locked on mine, showing her eagerness to hear more. "What is he like?"

My thoughts ran rampant with answers—handsome, attentive, kindhearted—my accolades could continue for hours on end. Instead, I chose a vague description.

"He is a pleasant young man." My hand brought my teacup to my lips, stifling the other words I wished to gush. Unfortunately, my pleasant thoughts about him could not remain hidden from the sparkle in my eye. Olivia instantly noticed my agreeable glimmer.

"You find him more than pleasant, I can see." She grinned. "Why is that?"

When the waitress approached with our order, I sighed in relief. Another opportunity to circumvent the discussion had presented itself.

"I'm famished," I replied, swiftly biting into the sandwich. With my mouth full, I would be safe from self-incrimination. My actions must have appeared comical because Olivia broke out laughing. After swallowing, I scowled. "What's so funny?"

"Why you, of course."

"Whatever do you mean?" Naturally, I knew she understood the reasons behind my actions.

"Grace, how long have we known each other?"

"A long time." I pouted, bracing for her reprimand.

"Then you know by now that I am familiar with your ability to ignore subjects, and that sandwich of yours will eventually be devoured, leaving your mouth empty and free to speak."

She was correct. I couldn't stuff it with food, tea, or even cakes for hours on end to avoid answering her questions.

"Very well." After dabbing my lips with my napkin, I looked sheepishly at her, feeling a flush fill my cheeks. "I admire Stefan Reyer. He is a wonderful brother, son, and . . ."

"And what?" Olivia leaned forward.

"Companion," I replied, choosing my words carefully.

My friend's mouth gaped open, and she set her teacup down in its saucer with a clink. "My God, Grace. You have fallen in love with him! I can see it in your eyes."

The recognition of my affections toward

Stefan caused me deep embarrassment. To be honest, I hadn't even admitted such strong emotions existed. His uncanny way of making me feel valued and adored had indeed incited a new sensation. It was that emotion Olivia had spoken of years ago. Suddenly Benedict came back into my mind.

"For heaven's sake," I replied. "I'm a married woman. How could you suggest such a thing?" My terse answer made me wince because I hated offending my dear friend.

"I'm not stupid," Olivia brashly replied. "You have not admitted in so many words that you are happy with your marriage either. In fact, I believe you to be miserable."

"Miserable?" For my sake, I should have scoffed at her observation but couldn't deny it.

"Tell me about Stefan," Olivia insisted. "What is it about him that has captured your sentiments so fiercely?"

For the life of me, as hard as I tried, I could not suppress my opinions any longer. Tears welled in my eyes as I admitted my fallen state.

"You have guessed correctly," I blubbered. "My heart is smitten with the lieutenant."

"Oh, dearest," Olivia replied softly. Her hand reached across the table and touched my weak flesh by my teacup. "Have you acted upon these emotions?"

Shaking my head negatively, I could at least be thankful I had not yielded to temptation. Nevertheless, I had thought about what it would be like in his embrace, kissing me with passionate desire, and taking me in romantic fervor. Already I had committed the act in my mind and no doubt sinned in doing so.

"Well, that's good news." Olivia sighed. "Does he feel the same as you do?"

With trembling lips, I answered, "I believe he does, but we are both careful not to articulate those sentiments. After all, we are under the scrutiny of his father and my mother-in-law, who has already chided me for spending far too much time in his presence."

"Yes, for proprieties' sake be careful, Grace. I do not wish to see your reputation ruined. When the war is over, he will return to Belgium. You know that, don't you?"

"Of course. I shall keep my girlish affections to myself. I'm sure when Benedict returns, this silly regard for the lieutenant will fade away into obscurity."

The notion of Stefan leaving had not occurred to me, reminding me of the cold reality that pursuing such affections was fruitless.

"Is he staying in the manor house?"

"No, no," I heartily replied, thankful he had not been. "He's in the hunting cabin about a mile away from the estate. Because of his leg injuries, he was unable to climb stairs."

"Well, just as well," Olivia agreed. The worry in her eyes appeared to dissipate.

Olivia ceased to press the matter further, and we enjoyed a leisurely lunch together, chatting about other subjects. Afterward, we strolled slowly back to her home. My driver had arrived to return me to the estate.

As we approached the door, Anna surprise-ingly opened it. However, a grin did not welcome us in return. Instead, a troubled expression had dulled her countenance as she held an envelope in her hand.

"This came for you while you were gone," she quietly announced, holding out the paper.

Olivia sucked in a sharp breath and flashed a petrifying gaze in my direction. When her eyes returned to the envelope, her voice trembled. "I cannot read it."

Anna's eyes begged me to take it, and I gathered the responsibility had fallen upon me to read the contents. Slowly I took it, noticing it had come from the War Office. My heart sank into the pit of my stomach as I broke the seal and pulled out the folded letter. The written words trembled as they left my mouth.

"Madam, it is my painful duty to inform you that a report has been received from the War

Office notifying the death of Private Thomas Gooding, which occurred in the field in Gallipoli. The report is to the effect that he was ..." I halted. "Perhaps you should read it," I said, holding it out to Olivia. She brought her hands to her mouth and stifled a sob.

"No ... no you," she begged with a quivering voice.

After gulping the lump in my throat, I continued slowly. "The report is to the effect that he was killed in action." My eyes watered as I continued the remaining condolences. "By His Majesty's command, I am to forward the enclosed message of sympathy from Their Gracious Majesties the King and Queen. I am at the same time to express the regret of the Army Counsel at the soldier's death in his country's service." Tears flowed down my cheeks as I gazed at the horrified expression on Olivia's face. I hesitated, took a breath, and continued. "I am to add that any information that may be received as to the soldier's burial will be communicated to you in due course. I am your obedient servant, H. B. Cooke, Second Lieutenant Officer in charge of records."

My cold fingers folded the paper and placed it back into the envelope. As soon as I did, Olivia's strength drained from her body, and she fell at my feet in inconsolable wails of sorrow. Both

Anna and I knelt down beside her, engulfing her in our embrace. As we held her in our arms, I never felt such dreadful anguish for another human being in my entire life.

Chapter 12

The Meaning of Grief

During my ride back to Stratton Park, I sat listlessly in the back seat of the car, staring at the passing scenery. My ears rang as if they still heard Olivia's cries from miles away. The pain of seeing her in such a state had torn my heart to shreds. Unexpectedly, the harsh reality of war had arrived upon Olivia's doorstep, stripping her of happiness and love. The consequences of the conflict could no longer remain a mere abstract out of sight or out of mind. Instead, the hideous truth of its penalties had arrived close to home.

As we approached the estate, I needed someone to talk to who understood. I leaned forward and spoke to the driver. "Take me to the cottage and drop me off. I need to speak to the lieutenant about an urgent matter."

Our chauffeur glanced at me in the rearview mirror with a raised brow, which I chose to ignore. If Florence discovered my whereabouts,

I would deal with her objections upon my return. At that moment, I needed the support of another human being I could trust. The only person I cared to express my painful thoughts to was Stefan.

The car pulled down the dusty road toward the cottage. As we approached and stopped, an anxious anticipation rose in my heart.

"Thank you," I addressed the driver somberly. "If Lady Russell inquires of my whereabouts, you may tell her I went for a walk upon my return and nothing more."

"Yes, my lady." He flashed a cautionary look.

Exiting the car, I closed the door and waited for him to pull down the road before approaching and standing before the entrance. After a brief knock, I heard Stefan's cane clap on the wooden floor and the familiar shuffle of his walk. As he swung open the barrier, my raw emotions eroded my composure with tears welling in my eyes.

"Lady Grace." His brows knit together as he scanned my face. "Something is wrong, what is it?"

Perhaps I should have surmised he thought I had received a telegram regarding Benedict's demise, but I only thought of Olivia's pain.

"Have you news of your husband?"

"My husband?" My heart pounded in my

throat. "No, it is my dear friend Olivia," my trembling voice countered. "She received a letter from the War Office that . . ." I could not say the phrase I had read an hour earlier. What did it mean? Had he been blown to pieces by a shell? Had a rifle bullet ripped through his heart? What terror had the poor man endured?

Stefan set both his hands upon my shoulders tenderly. "That he was killed in action."

My head shook affirmatively, and I felt such anguish for Olivia that my stomach soured. "My poor friend is so grief-stricken," I replied. "We went out for lunch, and when we returned, a letter had arrived."

"I'm so very sorry. Come in and sit." He took my hand in his and led me inside, closing the door behind me. Without protest, I followed him and sat on the couch.

"It was dreadful," I continued. "I had to read the terrible letter to her myself because she could not bear to read the words."

"There is no easy way to tell a family of such a loss," his empathetic voice replied. "Did they have children?"

"No, and perhaps that is for the best," I said. Having known they had tried for a child beforehand, what would Olivia have done with a young babe and now left a widow? On the other hand, perhaps it would have been comforting to have a part of Thomas she would always see in a child.

"It must frighten you."

Stefan's impulsive declaration confused me, and I scowled. "Frighten me? Why should it frighten me?" It took me a minute to correctly ascertain what he meant by the statement. To my shame, I suddenly realized he had been referring to my husband. "You mean Benedict." I gulped in embarrassment.

At the beginning of the war, I feared that one day we would receive dreadful news of his demise. As I pondered the possibility now while sitting in Stefan's presence, my fear had withered away to an agreeable acceptance should it happen to me. It was a terrible, thoughtless state of affairs to admit my sorrow would be minimal. It only confirmed my heart had fallen into a state of disenchantment because of my growing regard for Stefan. Admittedly, my affection turned toward him.

"No, I am not frightened," I responded calmly. "I can accept it should I receive news about Benedict." My cold tone declared it confidently with conviction.

"Grace."

My name fell from his lips with a sweetness that caused me to smile, and I took notice of the cautionary glint in his eyes.

"You know why, don't you, Stefan?"

He bit his lower lip in a worrisome gesture, pulling his gaze away from me. The actions of a gentleman remained poised next to me, but I had to know whether his heart had declared to him otherwise.

My hand extended and clasped his. "Do you care for me?"

Shocked by my question, he jerked at my touch. In his eyes, a deep longing spoke to me as if they expressed the sinful words I wished him to confess. "Tell me," I prodded him. "If I were your wife, what would you . . . what would you do?" He paused a bit as if he pondered the effect his words would have upon my heart.

"Then I should kiss you, my sweet Grace, and cherish our every moment together."

"Kiss me now," I entreated, squeezing his hand tighter. My heart yearned for him to act upon my plea, but instead, he merely stared at me, refusing my invitation. Naturally, my soul sank at the delay that spoke of his rejection or perhaps caution. Rather than belabor the uncomfortable moment between us, I released his hand and rose to my feet.

"How utterly selfish I am," I lamented, placing my hands over my face in embarrassment. "My dearest friend has lost her husband, and I entreat you like a risqué woman with no conscience."

Stefan stood to his feet. "You have no idea how I long to give you what you ask."

His hands took mine and tenderly pulled them away from my reddened cheeks. Mortified by my behavior, I felt compelled to escape. With a swift jerk, I pulled away and averted his gaze.

"I shall never ask again. Forgive me, Lieutenant."

Covered in shame, I departed in haste from the cottage, running away from my desperate need for affection. As I sprinted down the lane, I became aware that grief could come in many forms. The heartache I felt about Stefan had crushed any hope we could love one another.

After running until I had lost breath in my lungs, I stopped along the side of the road. In the distance stood the estate, shrouded by the gray clouds lingering above. As I deeply inhaled the air to catch my breath, a raindrop splattered on my left cheek. Lifting my head upward, I watched as small drops dripped one by one on my face, mingling with the tears of regret. My heart ached, thinking I would die never knowing the depth of true love or the passion Olivia had expressed in her joy with Thomas. At that moment, I understood she had lost much more than a husband. She had lost a lover, a companion, and the soul that mingled in harmony with hers.

The rain increased to a full shower, drenching my dress. Uncaring whether I would catch a chill or not, I slowly meandered down the dirt road back into the emptiness of my life.

Upon my return, I ran upstairs to change out of my wet clothing and toweled dry my hair. My emotions had turned cold as the chill and dampness of the fabric that clung to my body. A numbness enshrouded me as I thought of Stefan. His recuperation and eventual return to service would alleviate my pain. Once he departed, no reminder would remain of my unfulfilled desires. It was as it should be because I already had a husband whose responsibilities were to provide me those things.

As I returned downstairs, freshened and ready to face the household, Carter met me in the foyer.

"A post has arrived for you from the baron," he announced, handing me the envelope.

"Give it to his mother," I replied, refusing to take it in my hand. No doubt it would have contained nothing of personal interest that I cared to read. Not today.

"It's addressed to you personally, your ladyship."

Once again, Carter shoved it my direction, showing the addressee on the envelope.

Surprised it only contained my name and not his mother's, I took it out of curiosity. A slight worry crinkled my brow as I pondered why he had chosen to write me in private.

"Thank you, Carter," I replied. Wishing for an occasion of privacy, I walked to Benedict's study, closed the door behind me, and opened the envelope. It had been the first private thought my husband had cared to write me for almost a year. As I read his words, my hand trembled at the onslaught of allegations leaping from the page.

"Mother has written to me about the boarders you have brought into our home. She has expressed her concern that your frequent interaction with Lieutenant Reyer has caused the household staff and other guests to gossip. It appears that your actions have brought humiliation and concern to my mother. Needless to say, I am surprised and disenchanted at your behavior."

My heart thumped in my chest from anger and mortification as Benedict's words boldly confronted my conduct. Had it been that obvious to the staff and perhaps the Smits? Did they think I had been carrying on an affair of sorts with Stefan? To my shame, I admittedly wanted to fall into his arms and lose myself. Thankfully, he had more sense than I had and had taken great care not to cross the line. With anxiety, I continued to read.

"My absence no doubt has been difficult for you, of that I am sure. My commanding officer has agreed to a two-week leave, and I shall be returning within the fortnight to put matters in order."

Benedict scrawled his name at the bottom as if he were angry. It did not appear to be his usual neat penmanship, and the parting words of putting matters in order frightened me. The fact Florence had dared to pen to my husband such a harsh accusation angered me to the core. She had stabbed me in the back, and I would not be silent about her scheme to discredit me. After storming through the estate room by room, I found Florence in the solarium, tending to her foliage.

"How could you be so insensitive as to pen a letter to Benedict with innuendos regarding my behavior with the lieutenant?" I waved the letter in front of her face, seething at the woman who stood before me. Instead of acknowledging my heated arrival and pointed question, she stood ignoring me while she watered the plants. "Well?" I cried, attempting to arouse her from her indifferent stupor. After a few seconds, she turned and glanced at me with a malevolent smirk on her face.

"I know what you've been up to," she spat in

anger. "In fact, I'm aware that even an hour ago you were alone with the lieutenant against your better judgment." She paused while glancing at me suspiciously. "Am I right?"

My shoulders pulled back in a defensive stance. "I had just arrived from visiting Olivia and comforting her after receiving dreadful news that her husband had died in battle." My lips clasp shut as I attempted to come up with a plausible reason for going to the cottage. Florence responded before I could speak further.

"As I remarked before, not unexpected since he was a mere private and on the front lines." With cold regard, she turned back and continued her task. Unbeknownst to her, she had given me my excuse.

"That is precisely why I sought out the lieutenant to speak of the matter because I knew your response would be without an ounce of empathy." I sucked in a breath before spewing out the remainder of my thoughts. "It's bloody cruel!" My words had incited Florence in return.

"So you took it upon yourself to seek solace from another man while married to my son?" Her eyes grew dark and threatening. "I warned you repeatedly to stay away from the lieutenant."

"He has been nothing but a friend and a perfect gentleman in my midst. Absolutely nothing untoward has transpired between us."

"I refuse to discuss it any further with you, Grace. You can explain your actions to Benedict when he comes home on leave."

"You orchestrated this entire event, didn't you?"

"I said I'm done speaking of the matter."

The matter. Yes, it was a *matter* of sorts, but never would I admit to Florence that my affections tempted me to become a fallen woman. I had concluded while glaring at my mother-in-law that I had a bigger problem to contend with in the future—Benedict's return.

CHAPTER 13

THE HOMECOMING

Within two weeks' time, Benedict had returned from the front, sending us a telegram as to the time of his arrival at the train station. My relations with Florence remained strained, to say the least. Stefan and I had barely spoken except for polite conversation when he intermittently joined the household for dinner. He knew of Benedict's impending visit but said little regarding his return. As a result, our interaction lessened, which had been my fault and a cautionary measure taken on Stefan's behalf.

As I stood on the platform, waiting for Benedict's return, I shivered even though it had been a reasonably warm, early-autumn day. My nerves pricked like needles while waiting to see my husband, knowing inwardly my heart had committed adultery a thousand times over in my mind. Even now as I saw the train slowly approach from the north, my thoughts lingered on another man.

The hissing of the engine passed before me, leaving behind the disgusting odor of oil and steel. Everything in the country had deteriorated since the war began because funds were diverted from the infrastructure to the making of weapons and ammunition. The screeching of the metal wheels upon the track grated on my nerves, and I glanced to the right and left of the car doors flying open, releasing its passengers.

Straining to see Benedict above the crowd, I stood up on my tiptoes nervously glancing around. Suddenly a familiar voice from behind me called my name.

"Grace!"

My stomach knotted, and I froze. Unable to swing around in gleeful joy upon hearing Benedict's voice, I slowly turned my head and glanced over my shoulder. He was nearly upon me, causing me to spin around and face him. His haggard appearance shocked me as if he had aged ten years within one.

"Darling," he drawled. He put his arms around me and drew me toward his chest.

"Benedict." Instead of ardently embracing him in return, I felt helplessly void of affection and stood rigid with his arms around my body. My actions were despicable as if I had become a statue incapable of movement.

"I've missed you," he uttered.

He released me, and I forced a feigned smile. "You look so tired. We should get you home immediately so that you can rest."

"I am," he admitted with a moan.

"The driver is waiting," I announced, putting my arm around his as he offered it. His other hand carried a large leather suitcase, and he had slung a duffle bag over his shoulder.

"It feels good to be home," he admitted. "The air is so fresh. It's the first deep breath I've taken in months."

"What do you mean?" I asked, having just complained about the smell of a dirty train on the platform.

"I've done nothing but breathe the stench of gunpowder, filthy conditions, and rotting corpses longer than I care to admit."

His dreadful admission saddened me, bringing to the forefront the realism of war. I, on the other hand, had suffered nothing.

Benedict clung to me tightly, pulling me toward his side. When we arrived at the car and climbed inside, our driver enthusiastically welcomed him home.

"It is good to see you, sir," he greeted.

"Thank you. I'm glad to be home," Benedict replied with a faint smile.

As we settled into the back seat, my focus remained upon him and his apparent physical and emotional detriment. Without thinking otherwise, I felt compelled to tell him of Olivia's loss.

"You remember my friend Olivia?"

"Yes." He turned his head and gave me his full attention.

"She recently lost her husband in Turkey, of all places." Benedict took my hand and held it tenderly.

"I'm sorry to hear of it." He scowled. "We had news of the massive losses. It has been quite disheartening."

"We are not going to lose the war, are we?" The idea of Germans invading our land pulled the breath from my lungs.

"If I have anything to say about it, no." He confidently boasted. "Yes, we've lost battles, but the war to victory continues. We will fight as long as it takes. I can tell you the morale of the men in my company is of the same mindset. The bloody Germans will not set foot on English soil."

After gulping in a shaky breath, I responded, "That is good to know."

"How is Olivia doing?"

My surprise that he continued to show empathy for her plight sent a warmth of affection returning to my heart.

"As good as can be expected. The last we spoke, she had talked of going back to live with her parents. Her current boarder, however, will need to find housing."

"Boarder?"

"A Belgian refugee."

"Oh, I see." His smile quickly faded.

Afraid to speak on the contentious topic, I swiftly returned his attention elsewhere. "I'm sure Percy will be delighted to be in your arms, darling."

"How is the lad?"

"Growing. You'll barely recognize him. He started to walk, albeit he's a bit unsure of himself."

"Walk you say?" He brought his hand to his forehead. "My goodness, I'm sure he has. I've lost track of time."

The car pulled up to the estate, and I heard Benedict heave a deep sigh of relief. His eyes scanned the property as if he were looking at it for the first time. In his honor, the staff stood in a long line to welcome him home. Florence exited and grinned as the car rolled to a stop. The Smits stood in the doorway watching, but Stefan was nowhere in sight.

"Mother looks well," he remarked.

The driver opened the car door, and I exited with Benedict to follow. Carter quickly stepped forward.

"Welcome home, Major," he replied. "It is

good to have you back." Benedict stood proudly in his uniform and gave Carter a hearty handshake.

"Thank you, Carter." He glanced over at the staff. The men nodded and smiled a warm welcome while the female staff gave him a curtsy and grin. "Thank you for greeting me. So kind of you," he remarked. After taking a few steps forward, Florence approached him.

"My darling boy," she remarked. "Home at last."

"Yes, mother, home but not for long." He gave her a quick embrace and kissed her right cheek. I saw he noticed the Smits standing in the doorway.

"These are two of our Belgian guests," I announced. "Hugo and Gretta Smit."

"Pleasure to meet you," Benedict replied. "Mrs. Smit, my mother has written to me about your prime pastries to such an extent my mouth watered while standing in the trenches."

Gretta flashed a proud smile. "Whatever you would like me to bake for you, just let me know, Major."

"I can't remember the last time I had a sweet pastry melt on my tongue. It's been far too long."

Benedict walked indoors, lumbering in exhaustion. As we entered the foyer, he stopped, removed his hat, and glanced at mother and me.

"The others?"

"The lieutenant is residing in the cottage, and Doctor Reyer is at the hospital. They both should be here for dinner this evening," Florence announced in my stead.

"All right then," he replied, shooting me an uncomfortable glance.

"If you don't mind, I'm exhausted. I haven't slept in a decent bed in months, and all I care to do now is sleep for a few hours. Shall you two forgive me?"

"Absolutely, nothing to forgive," I responded. "Come, I'll help you get settled in." Tenderly I held Benedict's hand, but it felt cold to the touch. As we walked up the stairs, he pulled his hand from mine. Once inside our bedchamber, he closed the door behind him and shot an angry glare in my direction that took me by surprise.

"Now that we are alone, I want to know why your behavior has required my return home."

His change in physical demeanor frightened me. The affectionate moments of his return had suddenly turned cold and challenging.

"You are here because your mother has blown the situation out of proportion," I quipped. "There was no need to call you home to take care of matters." Defensively I stood my ground before him in hopes he would believe my explanation. Benedict beheld me warily, scanning my eyes.

"Who is this lieutenant?" The angry tone of his voice demanded an answer. "Has his conduct toward you been inappropriate, or have you merely thrown yourself into his presence as mother suggested?"

"Thrown myself?" I screeched. "What do you take me for, Benedict, some floozy? You know I've been nothing but faithful to you since the day we married. I have no intention of being unfaithful to you either."

"Then why spend so much time with the man? Mother tells me you have often been alone with him at the cottage. Such lack of propriety on your behalf is eliciting gossip and speculation that the two of you are having an affair."

"Affair?" A nervous giggle escaped my throat. "How preposterous." My stomach knotted as Benedict eyed me suspiciously. After a few seconds, his countenance softened. Suddenly I felt drenched in alarm as he took a step in my direction and lifted my chin.

"Look at me." He spoke kindly.

I reluctantly obeyed his command, and when our eyes met, instinctively I knew what would come next.

"Your husband needs his wife." Benedict lowered his mouth upon mine and kissed me fervently. The months of war that had denied him the body of a woman suddenly unleashed into a consuming fire of need. His lips remained on mine while his free hand clawed at my skirt, lifting it upward to search for my flesh underneath. In frustration, he crudely picked me up, placed me on the bed upon my back, and unzipped his pants releasing his bulging need before my eyesight. Overwhelmed, I shut my eyelids and cringed.

"Honestly, Benedict," I balked. "Can you not wait until we at least undress?"

"No," he said. "The wait has been far too long."

After awkward attempts to pull down my undergarments, Benedict entered me swiftly and let out a moaning cry I hoped none of the staff, or his mother, had heard. It had been so long between our last joining that his penetration hurt with each thrust. Knowing it would be wrong to halt his need after such a long time, I allowed him to have his way with me until he released himself with a groan of pleasure. It didn't take long to do so, and at that second, I felt sorry for him. I wasn't sure why, as he rolled off my body, heaving in gratification.

Embarrassed over my position, I swung my legs over the bed and sat on the edge, pulling up my undergarments and dealing with the raw pain of his return. Naturally, in the act, I again had received nothing in return. I wondered if Benedict even knew women had needs or if our duty in life had only been to spread our legs and receive a man for his inclinations alone. Frustration engulfed me as I rose to my feet and glanced down at his limp body lying on top of the bed.

"You should get undressed and sleep. I'm sure it will feel much better between clean sheets," I remarked, glancing at his dissipating arousal.

"You're right," he replied. "Wake me an hour before dinner."

"As you wish." I straightened my skirt, roaming the palm of my hands down the wrinkled front to make myself semipresentable. After glancing in the mirror and tucking in a few stray curls that had fallen out during the onslaught, I turned and watched him before departing. He stood on the other side of the bed with his back toward me, taking off his uniform. Not wishing to glance upon his naked body, I opened the door and left my returning soldier alone.

CHAPTER 14

THE HOSTILE ENCOUNTER

While Benedict slept peacefully in our bed, I anxiously anticipated the evening ahead. It was impossible to warn Stefan of the insinuations that had reached my husband. Unfortunately, I had no idea of the extent of his suspicions. Worried sick, I spent the majority of the afternoon watching the clock tick precariously close to their meeting.

As instructed, I returned to our bedchamber to awaken him and change for dinner but surprisingly found him already awake. He had bathed and dressed for the evening, changing into his dress uniform, wearing a red tunic with gold trim. Covered in his insignias and rank emblems, I gawked at the change in his appearance. Sleep helped to eradicate the dark circles beneath his eyes.

"Why are you not dressed in civilian clothes?"

"Because I'm in service, Grace. It's not proper." He flashed an irritated glance as if I should know the reason. "Besides, I believe your lieutenant will be joining us this evening for dinner. It's a matter of protocol."

Protocol? All I could think about was my husband had insisted on pulling rank on Stefan. Admittedly, Benedict looked formidable clothed in his uniform. A corner of my heart swelled with pride over his military achievements.

"All right then," I acquiesced, not wishing to pursue the discussion further. "I need to change for dinner as well."

Benedict strolled over to my closet and pulled back the hangers one by one. "I hope you don't mind, but I miss seeing you in this gown." He chose a dress with powder-blue silk satin bodice and lace, accented by a flowing, embellished chiffon shirt. He had always adored the dress, but I had not worn it in a few years and thought it out of style. Nevertheless, his actions furthered my suspicions he wished to reiterate his influence upon me as his husband.

"By all means. I'd be pleased to wear it if that is what you want," I replied, smiling at him in agreement.

"Good." Benedict turned and walked toward the door. "Now if you don't mind, I wish to find Mother and spend a few moments together with her before dinner."

My husband spending time alone with his mother increased my apprehension. Without having the knowledge of what lying tidbits she would feed him before meeting Stefan, my helplessness in the situation loomed before me.

After drawing a quick bath, I took time preparing to appease Benedict. When I had dressed and checked my hair for the last time, I stood and walked to the window. I could see our car arriving, delivering Stefan for dinner. Pulling back the curtain, I watched it slow to a stop and witnessed Stefan get out, fully dressed in uniform as well. His handsome appearance and youth would not sit well with Benedict—of that I felt sure. A battle of another sort brewed in the household, and with trepidation, I made my way downstairs to face the evening between the two men in my life.

Upon hearing voices in the parlor, I entered relieved to see everyone had arrived. The Smits stood near Benedict, appearing to have an amicable discussion. Stefan remained by his father, having a quiet conversation while Florence turned and shot a nasty glare in my direction. She had the innate ability to make sure only my eyes saw her actions and not her son's, who nodded his head over something that Hugo said. Suddenly Celia bounced into the room, with her curls bobbing up and down. Her usual antics of screaming her brother's name and running into his arms played out before everyone.

"Stefan, you look handsome in your uniform," she gushed.

"Celia, tone down your excitability. We are honored with the presence of Major Russell, who is on leave for a visit."

Celia spun around and looked at Benedict. She narrowed her eyes at him and innocently asked a question. "Is my brother the lieutenant a higher rank than you?"

Benedict grinned with a sly glint in his eyes. "Perhaps you should ask your brother, young lady."

My spine stiffened at the blatant innuendo to make sure Stefan acknowledged his place in the room. Celia grabbed Stefan's hand. "Well, are you Stefan? You're bigger than him, right?"

"I'm afraid not," he swiftly answered, seemingly unembarrassed. "A major would be senior in rank, Celia."

A major. I stifled a giggle at his response. Instead of acknowledging him as the higher-ranking officer, the roundabout response spoke volumes. Doctor Reyer apparently felt compelled to clarify and spoke up.

"The major is in the British Army, while your brother here is a Belgian carabineer. They are two different countries and branches of service."

Celia, appearing more confused than before her query, shrugged her shoulders. "Well, okay then."

"Belgian carabineers." Benedict spoke solemnly. "Your father mentioned before your arrival that you had fought at Liege."

"That is correct, sir," Stefan replied with a proud gaze. "I hope to return to continue the resistance and halt further territorial occupation by the Germans."

"After that leg of yours is fully healed," Doctor Reyer clarified.

"Soon, I hope," Benedict replied coldly, obviously making a point for my sake he wished him out of our home and far from me.

"Well, it strengthens every day, and I'm anticipating no more than a few more weeks of recuperation."

"Can we not speak of war this evening?" Hastily, my voice interjected. "Just once I'd like to have a quiet evening of polite conversation away from the subject."

"My wife has a point," Benedict said, coming to my side. "I for one need to put aside the battlefield and focus on more pleasant tasks while I'm here."

The pleasant task had undoubtedly referred to bedding me during the next weeks, and once again, he made the statement to make a point. I shot a nervous glance at Stefan, who appeared uncomfortable with the thought as much as I did.

Florence caught my wandering gaze, taking in my indiscretion. Thankfully, Carter announced dinner, and we made our way into the dining room.

Being on the arm of Benedict felt strangely foreign as he escorted me toward the table. His familiarity I once enjoyed no longer existed. Instead, my wicked heart consistently drew its wandering affections toward Stefan only a few feet away. I felt helplessly drawn but for what purpose? Had I merely fantasized this younger man held the answers to my unfulfilled desires? As I ruminated over my miserable state of affairs, Benedict leaned toward me and whispered.

"You look lovely this evening, Grace. Thank you for wearing the dress." His heartfelt comment brought my mind back to where it should have been—to my husband.

"Anything for you," I replied, smiling at him. Suddenly Florence directed an odd question.

"Lieutenant, do you have a young lady back home that has captured your fancy?"

My mouth gaped open at the meddling question she posed before everyone, causing an apparent humiliation to Stefan by the look on his face.

"Thankfully, no," he said. "If I had a loved one trapped in Belgium at this time, it would be most distressing to think of the hardships and dangers she might endure during my absence."

Having read of the despicable Germans raping women in the country with no thought of guilt whatsoever, I understood his remark.

"Well, indeed when the war has ended, you'll marry and settle down and be as happy as my son and Grace are together." Florence smiled at the two of us as I seethed at her underhanded ploy.

"Stefan, if you find a girl, you need to make sure she will fly a kite with me like Grace."

"You've been kite flying?" Benedict raised a brow.

"Celia and I have been playing all sorts of things while she's been here, haven't we, dear? We've mended her doll too." I didn't wish her to go into details regarding the kite-flying episode, so I steered her direction elsewhere.

"Celia, I'm afraid, needs more attention than I can provide her at the moment," Doctor Reyer clarified. "I'm most grateful for Lady Grace and the thoughtfulness she has given my daughter."

"I see," Benedict replied. "That reminds me, Grace. I stopped by the nursery to see Percy before speaking with Mother. He's a fine lad and has grown more than I expected."

"Babies do those sorts of things . . . grow," I replied with a smirk. Benedict's eyes softened into a soulful gaze.

"Well, perhaps it's time for another child."

The announcement at the dinner table embarrassed me. How could he bring up such a subject in front of our guests without any qualms? By the knowing twinkle in his eye, I surmised once again it to be a maneuver on his part to solidify the importance of our union for Stefan's sake. His actions confirmed to me Benedict felt threatened by the younger man at his table, and he surmised that Stefan had captured my fancy whether I admitted to it or not.

"A topic to discuss in private, dear." I gleefully chuckled, acting entertained by his comment.

Eventually the discussion changed to trivial subjects as the Smits and Doctor Reyer joined in. Stefan spoke quietly to the others, appearing aloof toward Benedict and me. After dinner had finished, the gentlemen retired alone for port and cigars while I stayed with Celia, Florence, and Gretta. My stomach balled into a knot, frightening me that I would expel my dinner at any moment. My mother-in-law appeared to enjoy my discomfort.

"Are you all right, Grace? You're looking pale."

"I'm all right," I responded. "Something at dinner didn't agree with me."

"The fish was a bit undercooked," Gretta

remarked. "That may be why you feel a bit queasy."

"Yes, I'm sure that's why." The dinner had nothing to do with it. It was the fact that the men were off alone talking among themselves. Inwardly I prayed Benedict would not make a fool of himself while in their presence. Certainly, he would have more sense.

About a half hour later, they entered the room. After a quick glance at Benedict, Stefan appeared anxious to leave. My suspicions were correct.

"If you don't mind, I'll walk back to the cottage tonight," he announced. "I could use the exercise."

"But your leg," I protested aloud, making my sentiments known. As soon as the words left my mouth, I cringed.

"He will do fine," Doctor Reyer assured me. "I examined him yesterday, and the bone has healed nicely. The muscles need exercising and strengthening before he returns to duty."

"Well then, if you'll excuse me," he said. "Ladies, good evening."

Celia naturally ran for a goodbye hug. "I wish you would stay." She pouted.

"It's about your bedtime anyway, isn't it?"

"I suppose." After giving her a hug, he headed toward the door.

"Let me see you out," Benedict offered in a firm tone.

By the sound of his voice, I knew it would not be a friendly farewell. As they left the room, my hands grew clammy as I clutched them in worry. A moment later, I begged my leave.

"Please forgive me," I hastily announced. "I'm not feeling well."

Escaping any forthcoming comments about my swift exit, I left the parlor and strode through the foyer to glance out the door. Benedict stood outdoors in front of Stefan in an authoritative stance. I neared but stayed hidden so I could hear their conversation.

"Stay the hell away from my wife," Benedict growled in a menacing tone.

"Contrary to what you may have heard, nothing immoral has transpired between Grace and me."

"You mean Lady Grace. I don't appreciate the familiarity in your tone. It's disrespectful."

My eyelids shut tight afraid to listen as they sparred with one another. A part of me wanted to run outdoors and stand between the two of them.

"With all due respect, Major, your wife only wants one thing."

"How in the hell do you know what my wife wants?" Benedict bellowed in return. "Stay the bloody hell out my private affairs."

Stefan remained silent and then replied in a low tone. Unable to hear what he had to say, it was impossible not to discern Benedict's immediate response to his comment. I heard the blow of his fist hit Stefan's jaw, and I glanced out the door to witness him fall on his back. It took every ounce of strength to restrain myself from running to him.

"I suppose I deserved that," he replied.

"Go back to the front where you belong and stay out of my affairs, you goddamn foreigner."

Afraid Benedict would discover I had heard the conversation and seen its violent end, I sprinted up the staircase to our bedchamber. Unable to hold back my emotions, tears trickled down my cheeks, falling onto the blue satin bodice. A moment later, Benedict stormed into the room, rubbing his knuckles.

"What did you do?" I yelped.

"What do you think I did? I hit the bastard to make a point."

"Why must you be so cruel to the man? I've told you nothing has happened between us."

"You think me stupid? I can see the way you look at him. You're in love with him, aren't you?"

"No, of course not." My trembling voice denied the accusation.

"You are forbidden to see him alone again, do you hear me, Grace? I don't need to be fighting a war on the front and fearful that behind my back you are unfaithful."

His cruelness caused me to bring my hands to the side of my head in disbelief. Heaving in anger, I railed in return. "Your mother put those thoughts into your head. She hates me, and all she is doing is meddling in our marriage."

"Keep my mother out of this," he spat with flaring nostrils. He unbuttoned his jacket and slipped out of it, throwing it on the chair. The heated argumentative situation had been our first. We had never argued with such intensity. It pricked my heart it had come to this dividing moment between us, and a wave of guilt washed over me.

"I will not be unfaithful to you, Benedict." My voice remained calm as I reassured him.

"It doesn't matter what you feel for him because, in ten days, he will be gone and back to his unit." He shot me a disgusting look. "Your childish crush will have dissipated, and that will be the end of it." He turned away from me and started to take his shirt off.

"Don't be angry with me," I pleaded. "I cannot bear you to be mad at me."

Ignoring me, he continued to undress. Benedict had been accurate in his assessment of my emotional state. Soon Stefan would be gone, and it would end. My life would return to being a dutiful wife. The course I had set for myself years ago at the matrimonial altar would not change. Perhaps it was nothing more than a childish crush.

Slowly I made my way toward him. "Will you help me out of the dress?" I asked, turning my back toward him. As I did so, I pulled out the comb holding my hair in place and let it cascade down my back. He remained silent. "Well?" I prodded him.

His fingers tenderly unbuttoned the dress. When he finished, he slipped it off my shoulders and started kissing my bare flesh. For the moment, I had drawn him back to me with the enticement of satisfaction and resigned myself to the forthcoming unfulfilling moment of intimacy.

CHAPTER 15

WOMEN OF BRITAIN SAY – "GO!"

Benedict's leave days melted away until once again the time to depart had arrived. He had spent his two-week respite with his son, mother, and I as if he cherished each moment being home. I could not blame him for doing so because of what awaited his return. More often than he had done so before the war, he sought my body. In respect and honor, I performed my conjugal duties, accepting the reality of our marriage.

Stefan had all but disappeared, keeping cloistered at the cottage and taking his meals there each evening instead of joining us for dinner again. His father must have heard about the incident, and he too stayed away, working late hours at the hospital.

When the day arrived for Benedict to return to duty, it felt as if the scene we had lived through a little over a year ago repeated itself. The same goodbyes with his mother at home occurred, and the same silent journey to the train station followed.

As I stood on the platform, waiting to say farewell, my eyes fell upon the posters tacked on the walls of the station. One of them showed a wife and children at the window of their home. Outside were men marching to war. The words "Women of Britain say—"GO!" were printed across the picture, supposedly representing patriotic sacrifice. As wives, we were to encourage the men in our lives to fight for country and king. The advertisement offended me because no woman in her right mind would willingly inspire her husband to walk toward death. To my shame, since the war's declaration, I had forgotten why we even were in this conflict. The onset and its political reasons made no sense to me. It seemed pointless.

My focus returned to Benedict as we came to a standstill before his coach. I threw my arms around his neck and gave him a tight hug. He deserved the show of affection even if no swelling of passionate love filled my heart. My husband was one of those men in the poster, marching into hell, and I hated it.

"Take care of yourself, Benedict." My voice trembled as I pulled away.

"As best I can," he replied.

His lips met mine with a glancing kiss, and I sensed an underlying worry in his actions.

"Percy will miss you," I said, smiling. "He is

such a darling boy, isn't he?"

"Indeed he is." A broad smile replaced the brooding look on his face. "I do love the lad."

"Do you love me?" I have no idea why I asked except I wondered if the recent events had dampened his affections. He pondered silently before answering.

"Of course I do," he said in an assuring voice. He brought his hand to the side of my cheek. "You know I do."

The yearning in his gaze told me he wanted my affirmation as well, which I readily gave. "I love you." My confession sounded insincere even in my hearing, and I feared Benedict sensed the words lacked depth. Perhaps he wanted to regain my whole heart because the day would come when Stefan would leave, and that would be the end of it.

The whistle loudly blew, causing me to jolt, and the conductor bellowed, "All aboard."

"Goodbye, my love." Benedict gave me a quick embrace. He turned and left, but his words had a definite finality in them that startled me.

A terrible fear of impending loss gripped my heart. Before I could say or do anything more, he disappeared and the train pulled out of the station. If it hadn't been for this damnable war, none of this would have happened. There would have been no goodbyes. The Belgian families would not have arrived. Stefan would have never captured my heart that belonged to another. Olivia would still have her husband. My fear and anger overwhelmed me until I staggered in my stance unable to control my balance.

"Are you all right, miss?" An elderly gentleman came to my side and grabbed my arm, giving me stability.

"Thank you," I replied. "Feeling a bit faint."

"Saying goodbye to your husband, I see."

"Yes, again."

"Sad days these are," he groaned. "Lost my only grandson last month."

Death was everywhere, and my lower lip quivered. "My condolences," I offered. "Yes, these are sad days indeed." After regaining the strength in my legs, I left the gentleman and returned to the car to resume my position as Lady Grace and count the days until my goodbyes to Stefan would painfully arrive.

The repeated scene reminded me of my neglectfulness toward Olivia. She had recently left her flat and returned home but in doing so found housing for Anna and her daughter. With Thomas gone, she found no purpose in staying at their marital home surrounded by the fond memories of their marriage, now destroyed by the war. With Benedict's leave and my selfish pursuits, I had not spoken to Olivia since that terrible day.

At my instruction, the driver took me to her parents' estate not far from my own. Olivia would be closer now, and I determined in the months ahead to rekindle our friendship. Spending time with her would fill the void, albeit I could not compare my own to her terrible loss.

Although my visit was unplanned, I saw relief on her mother's face upon my arrival.

"Grace, you have no idea how timely your call is today," she said, grabbing my hands.

"I'm sorry I have not visited since Olivia's return, but I felt compelled to see her today." I glanced about looking for her, but she was nowhere in sight. "How is she, might I ask?"

"Dreadfully melancholy, I'm afraid."

"I'm not surprised." Naturally, Olivia's grief would continue for some time.

"I had no idea," her mother said, "how much she loved Thomas."

"She was fortunate to find such an incredible man but so unlucky to have it cruelly taken away."

"Go talk to her, Grace. She will listen to you. She's up in her bedroom."

"I'll do what I can," I offered.

Her circumstances had taken her full circle home to the bedchamber we played in together as young girls. When I approached the closed door, I stood silently asking heaven above for wisdom. After a quiet knock on the door, I heard her voice.

"Come in."

When I turned the doorknob and crossed the threshold, I felt unprepared to deal with what I saw. Olivia had lost weight, and her natural rosy complexion looked like chalk. She appeared as if she hadn't eaten or slept in weeks.

"Grace," she said, forcing a smile. "You came to visit."

"I'm sorry it's been so long since we last spoke. I've been remiss in not checking on you sooner." I gave her a hug, and my friend clung to me tightly for a few moments. When she pulled away, my heart broke seeing tears well in her eyes.

"Sweet, sweet Olivia, what have you done to yourself?" I sympathetically asked. A slight puff of air escaped her pursed lips.

"I don't care if I live or die. Each day I wish I could be with Thomas."

Her lower lip quivered, and I knew she meant every word of it. After taking her hand, I pulled her toward the edge of the bed. We both sat down, and I placed my arm around her waist.

"Thomas would not approve." I tried not to sound accusatory. More than anything, I wanted to give her hope for a future. "He would want you to dry your tears, cherish the love you shared, but find strength and encouragement to build a happy life in his memory."

"How can I be happy?" she protested. "He was the love of my life, Grace, and now he's gone. I can't even visit his grave and leave flowers. The men who died in Gallipoli are buried in the fields in which they fell and left there for eternity. It's so cruel."

"War is cruel," I responded. "Thomas fought bravely, Grace, of that I'm sure. No doubt you were the last thing on his mind before he left this world." After brushing her wet curls from her cheek, I smiled at her warmly. "He would want you to be happy. You need to start eating and get rest."

Olivia lowered her face into the palm of her hands. Watching her deal with the loss of the man she loved incited me to declare my self-centered dilemma.

"I just came from taking Benedict to the station."

Olivia swiftly lifted her head. "You mean he came home?"

"Yes, on leave for two weeks."

"Oh, how wonderful for you, Grace, to be able to see him."

"For the most part, yes, but not all of it turned out to be pleasant, I'm afraid."

"What do you mean?"

Olivia sat upright and gave her attention to me. Perhaps it would help get her mind off her grieving woes if I confessed mine.

"He punched the lieutenant in the jaw."

"Oh dear, why?"

"Well, I blame it on his mother. You know she can be a meddling witch when she puts her mind to it." Relaying the story, I became exuberant. "She had the audacity to write to Benedict, suggesting I might be having an affair with Stefan. That was the sole reason he asked for leave to come home and take care of matters as he put it."

My friend's eyes grew wide, and I swiftly acted to clarify the falsehood of the accusation.

"You can be assured I have not been unfaithful to Benedict," I said. Then my brow crinkled as I thought of the truth of the matter. "Well, not physically anyway, but I cannot deny I've fantasized about it." Naturally, I expected Olivia to scold and warn me as she had done before. She sat there studying me for a few moments in silence and then reached out and grabbed my hand.

"Have you fallen in love with him, Grace? The lieutenant, I mean."

The question haunted me continually. Whatever emotion I felt for Stefan, it had been far different from my sentiments for Benedict. I had spent so much time examining the inner workings of my heart that I could not discern where I stood on the matter. Perhaps I loved them both but in different ways.

"I honestly do not know," I replied. "Oh, Olivia, I do like him so and have often pondered since his arrival if I shortchanged myself by marrying Benedict. I married for my convenience if nothing else and always held him in high regard. You know that I do."

Olivia shook her head. "Of that I am sure, Grace, but you haven't experienced the totality of love even though he is your husband."

"On the other hand, I dream about it with Stefan so often. I even asked him to kiss me, but he was such a gentleman that he refused."

"Doesn't he feel the same about you?"

"I'm sure he does, but he is honorable and has not crossed that line." I smirked. "You know, I oozed with green envy when I heard you speak of your intimate love and enjoyment with your husband. Even though he is gone now, you were so lucky to have experienced such a beautiful relationship when he was alive."

"I know I shall never love another as I loved him," she confessed.

"Do you promise me for his sake and your own that you will start eating again and find peace so that you can rest?"

"I'll try." Her shoulders slouched once again.

"Good then." I heaved in relief. "I'm sorry, dearest, but I must get back to Stratton Park."

Olivia rose to her feet and gave me a hug. She opened her mouth to speak but then hesitated. By the look in her eyes, I knew she wanted to say something but felt reluctant to do so.

"What is it?" I asked. She lowered her head for a brief second and returned her gaze to me.

"If I've learned anything, Grace, is that this war gives no promise to return those we love. Benedict may never come home, and Stefan may never return once he leaves."

"Yes, I know," I painfully admitted to myself.

"As your friend, I would never encourage you to be unfaithful to your husband, but . . ."

"But what?"

"But if you have indeed fallen in love with the lieutenant, then you must grab what you can of the few moments of joy it may bring you. Tomorrow holds no promise for anyone."

The moral advice given before had diminished. In Olivia's advice, though not so plainly stated, she suggested not to let my chance to experience what I had dreamed about slip away.

"I understand."

After giving her a long hug and a goodbye

kiss on her cheek, I left Olivia alone in her room. I hoped she would take my guidance to eat and sleep while cherishing the precious memories of her husband.

As I returned home, Olivia's words to grab my chance for happiness stirred my desires to be free. Whatever that meant, I only knew it frightened me, causing me to examine my loyalty to my husband. The days were slipping away like sand between my fingers. Stefan would soon leave, and I would never see him again.

CHAPTER 16

THE DARK AND THE LIGHT

As the days drew closer to Stefan's departure, my private conflict increased tenfold. I lay on my back in bed, staring at the ceiling, wrestling within to make a choice. Perhaps it had been the full moon streaming through my bedroom window fiercely tempting me as the minutes passed. Whether the moonlight had bewitched me, I couldn't tell when I eventually acted upon my impulses.

Hastily I slipped into a casual red dress I rarely wore, grabbed a shawl for the cold night air, and tiptoed down the stairs. A moment later, I slipped out into the dark of night a few minutes after twelve o'clock, unseen by Stratton Park's all seeing eyes, and began a mile-long walk down the dusty road to the cottage.

The crisp night air filled my nostrils, and a slight breeze chilled me. It didn't matter because the landscape morphed into a breathtaking sight under the light of the bright moon. No fear gripped my heart as I walked in the dark—only anticipation drew me forward until I reached the cottage. With a knuckle rap upon the door, I must have startled Stefan from sleep. I heard the rustling and shuffle of his feet.

"Who's there?" he shouted, sounding somewhat alarmed.

Not expecting a midnight guest, I quickly calmed his fears that a dangerous stranger stood on the other side of the door.

"It's me, Stefan," I called out.

A second later, the door flew open to reveal him standing in a white undershirt and his army trousers. His suspenders lay dangling at his sides.

"For goodness' sake, Grace, what are you doing here at this hour?"

My heart beat thunderously with such desire I thought I would swoon at his feet. I didn't have the words to answer him rationally, but I knew if I showed Stefan why I had come to his doorstep in the dead of night, he would understand. With trembling arms, I embraced him, met his lips with mine, and took the kiss I had longed to experience since the moment he arrived at Stratton Park. He belonged to me, and I seized the moment with an ardent appetite.

Without prudent objection, Stefan took me in his arms in return. All of his unspoken affections poured into my soul like sweet, intoxicating wine. An astounding sensation of melting together as one overtook me, and whether it was right or wrong, he understood what I wanted. His lips pulled away from mine, and he earnestly searched my eyes.

"Are you sure you want to do this?"

"Yes, it's why I came."

"But what of your husband?"

"What of him? It's you that I love, Stefan. Everything I should have waited for in life, I have found in you. Please, don't leave England forever without making love to me." My voice trembled, and for a brief moment I feared he would deny me once again. A small smile curled the corner of his lips, and his adoring blue eyes spoke of his love in return.

"You have no idea how I have longed for you, my sweet, sweet Grace."

No words could describe the heated desire that traveled through my veins upon hearing his declaration. An awareness of aching hunger engulfed me. A moment later, Stefan and I undressed each other and then clung as one. Aroused as I had never been before and handled by the hands of passion, I had arrived at an unknown place I longed to experience. A second later, he picked me up, laid me on the bed, and touched me tenderly in places I had not thought could elicit such blissful pleasure. The drought of the unknown became drenched in desire, and I experienced the elusive ecstasy spoken of by Olivia.

Perhaps I should have felt guilty for committing adultery with such lack of regard, but in all probability, I would never see Stefan again once he left for the front. With utter abandonment, we made love and poured our bodies and souls into each other. We both knew this had been fate and perhaps the only time together we would ever know. Determined to satisfy my thirst, I savored every blissful minute, experiencing the meaning of passionate love.

Afterward, we lay in each other arms, clinging to one another. My joy threatened to turn into sorrow as I realized the minutes were evaporating between us.

"I can't bear the thought of your leaving," I whispered. Stefan stroked my back, comforting my distress.

"Let us not think of it now," he replied. "But cherish our time with each other."

It was painful to admit we could never be together. Benedict would undoubtedly return after the armistice arrived, and Stefan would live with his father and sister to rebuild their country and home in Belgium. My mediocre life would resume as Lady Grace, wife to Benedict and mother to Percy, living out the decision I had made years ago to marry for convenience and not love. My destiny would be to grieve for eternity the inability to be with the man who brought me unbridled joy.

As the night drew near to morning, I hastened to return to the estate before being discovered missing by Florence or the staff. Dressing in haste, I gazed at Stefan lying on his back in bed. With his head propped up on a pillow, an endearing grin curled his lips. A sheet draped over the lower portion of his body.

"You have a beautiful figure," he remarked. "One that I shall fondly remember while in the trenches."

"Trenches," I moaned. Even though I had no idea what a trench looked like, the notion of men digging holes in the earth for safety repulsed me. The horrors of war frightened me. "Promise me you won't get yourself shot again."

He jumped out of bed and drew me close. "There are some things in life, my sweet, which men have no control over. Whether the bullets fly past me or into me, only God knows my destiny in the days ahead."

"Perhaps, but God never asks women our opinion on the matter. We are left, like Olivia, to suffer heartbreak when they are cruelly taken."

"Those we love?" He cocked his head and chuckled.

"Yes, those we love as I love you." After

throwing my arms around his neck, I kissed him again.

"And I you, my precious Grace," he whispered after our lips parted. "Fate has given us these moments together for a reason. Let us not grieve over our parting but be thankful for our time together."

A tear trickled down my cheek as he spoke the words and held me in his arms. I glanced out the window and panicked seeing the breaking dawn. "I must leave," I replied, grabbing my shawl and throwing it around my shoulders. "Goodbye, Stefan."

Afraid my sin would find me out, I sprinted out the door and ran down the dirt road toward home but not without one last look over my shoulder. Stefan stood in the doorway, waving goodbye. It was a memory I would undoubtedly carry until the day I died.

Out of breath and fearful, I quietly returned. Unseen by anyone, I sprinted up the staircase but halted upon hearing the wailing cries of my son in the nursery down the hall. His high-pitch voice brought concern, and without hesitation, I entered his room to find the nanny holding him in her arms and pacing the floor.

"What's wrong?" When I approached and saw his reddened face, my concern grew to alarm.

"He has a fever," she replied. "He woke only

a few minutes ago crying, and I came in haste to tend to him."

"Fever? From what?"

"I do not know, my lady."

Without hesitation, I sprinted down the hall and knocked incessantly on Doctor Reyer's door.

"Yes, yes, coming." I heard his voice and the floorboards creak as he approached. The door swung open. "What is it?" His bushy brows crinkled together.

"My son," I gasped. "He has a fever. Would you be so kind as to tend to him?"

"Yes, indeed," he said. "Let me get my robe on and grab my bag."

As I ran to the nursery to wait for Martin, the door to Florence's room flung open, followed by the Smits and a yawning Celia, rubbing her eyes. If Percy's cry wasn't enough to send me into a frenzy, curious eyes outside the door didn't help. Naturally, Florence pushed her way into the scene clad in her nightgown.

"What is going on here?"

"Percy isn't feeling well," I calmly replied, keeping my panic under check. Glancing at Celia and the Smits, I pleaded. "Please, go back to your rooms and back to bed. Everything is under control here."

Celia quickly obeyed after her father gave her a nod to do as told. The Smits nodded in agreement and returned to their room, closing the door behind them. Doctor Reyer made his way into the nursery and took Percy from Jane's arms.

"Come here, little fellow," he consoled, laying him down in his crib. "Let's have a look."

Percy wailed while Martin examined him. Florence came and stood by my side, her face drawn with concern as my own.

"What is it, Martin?" Florence stepped closer.

"Give him space, Florence, to examine Percy," I scolded her, grabbing her by the arm and halting her approach. She scowled back at me, noticing my attire and unkempt hair.

We both watched as Martin examined my son with a furrowed brow. When he lifted Percy's nightgown, I gasped as I saw a distinct red rash on his torso.

"What is that?" Unable to control myself, I stepped forward, pushing my way past Florence.

"I'm not sure," he said, shaking his head. "There have been cases of measles reported of late."

Suddenly Nanny Jane gasped. "My nephew had a bad case," she said, "when I went to visit him last week on my afternoon off."

"You visited a sick child and then came back here infecting Percy?" Florence screamed.

"No, now don't go accusing the nanny,"

Doctor Reyer said. "Unless she is infected too, there is no way she could have carried the disease except if Percy had been exposed to other children."

"Has he?" It was my turn to scowl at the nanny.

"No, no, I would never put him in harm's way such as that, my lady."

"It's too early to tell what the lad has except a fever. The rash could very well be a heat rash and nothing more." He closed his bag and spoke to Florence with a reassuring voice. "Let's keep an eye on him."

As I went and hovered over Percy's crib, gazing at my son who looked more like his father with each passing day, guilt washed over me. For the past hours, I had made passionate love to another man, and now my son lay ill. Had God decided to punish me for my sinful actions? Fearful at the possibility, I took charge of the moment.

"Then I will stay by his side," I firmly declared, "and watch over him." It didn't matter I was exhausted, having not slept the entire evening. "Please go," I ordered everyone in the room, wanting to be alone.

"I'll stay with you, my lady," Nanny Jane said, looking at me sorrowfully.

"No, you will not."

"Let me know if you need me," Florence said. She walked over and gazed at Percy. "Poor child. Perhaps it's nothing more than the sniffles." She sighed.

"Possibly." Doctor Reyer replied, and at that second I thought the man incompetent of diagnosing any illness.

They both left and closed the door behind them, leaving me alone as I had insisted. Tears burst from eyes as my pent-up emotions released. Guilty yes, but sorrowful no. I had experienced the love and passion I had craved for years only to realize I would never know it again.

CHAPTER 17

BACK TO THE TRENCHES

The next morning, I awoke, slumped in a chair by Percy's crib. My neck, stiff from having bent it uncomfortably, pained me as I moved. My eyes focused, and I looked at Percy. Thankfully, he slept peacefully. When my hand touched his forehead, relief flooded my heart that he was no longer burning up from fever. However, by his loud breathing, his nostrils had filled with mucus as a discharge rolled down his upper lip.

"Thank God, nothing more than a bad case of sniffles." I sighed, taking my hankie and dabbing away the secretion. After, I lifted his cotton nightshirt and discovered the rash had lessened. A soft knock came at the door, and a moment later Nanny Jane entered, looking sheepishly at me as if she were guilty of everything we threw at her hours earlier.

"How is he?"

"The fever has broken," I replied. "He looks and sounds as if it's only a common cold."

"Oh, thank the Lord above." She heaved in relief, bringing her hand to her chest.

"Would you mind watching him now? I'm afraid I'm exhausted."

"Yes, my lady, my pleasure."

Still clad in the garments I had stripped from my body when seeing Stefan, I wearily walked to my bedchamber. Florence, coming up the staircase, halted me with a call.

"Grace, how is my grandson?"

Slowly I faced her and forced a calm tone. "He's much better. The fever has broken, and he apparently has the sniffles and nothing more."

"Well, that is good news indeed," she replied. Florence stood looking at me curiously. "I meant to ask you why you were dressed this morning. You looked disheveled and out of sorts."

"I couldn't sleep," I quickly replied. "It was a night of tossing and turning, so I grabbed a dress and went down to the kitchen for a cup of tea."

"Oh, I see," she remarked suspiciously. Her eyes narrowed at me as if she pondered my truthfulness in the matter.

"Please excuse me, Florence, but I'm exhausted and wish to lie down for a while."

"All right," she replied, pushing past me in the hallway. "I'll check on Percy."

Satisfied she suspected nothing had been amiss over my behavior, I returned to my room for a few hours of sleep. However, rest eluded me as the minutes passed one by one, replaying in my mind the moment I had arrived at the cottage. The sensation of his touch and his ardent lovemaking continued to fuel my body. Fighting the urge to run back to him, I rose, bathed, and changed my clothes.

When I arrived downstairs, I jolted at hearing the voice of Stefan in the parlor. While rounding the doorway, my heart sank as I witnessed him fully clothed in his uniform and a duffle bag by his side. His words sent a searing heat of pain through my heart as he stood before Florence and the Smits. Celia stood by his side, clinging to him tightly. Fresh tearstains streaked her cheeks.

"Before I leave, I need to thank you for your hospitality," Stefan said. He looked at Florence with a sincere glint of gratitude in his eyes. "If it hadn't been for the peacefulness of the cottage setting, I don't think I would have recovered as quickly as I did."

Florence caught sight of me standing in the doorway. "I'm sure my daughter-in-law will agree that we are most grateful for your appreciation."

"You're leaving?" The words flew from my lips without thought as I trembled at the sight.

"Yes, Lady Grace. I received word this morning to report back to my unit."

"So soon?" I meant to say so soon after our intimate lovemaking. How could he merely pack and leave after what had transpired only hours earlier? Had he known of it beforehand? Question after question whirled in my mind, and my face contorted in distress. Florence narrowed her eyes at me as if she understood my near emotional breakdown.

"I'm afraid so," he said. "Thank you again for your hospitality."

"You are more than welcome, Lieutenant," Florence remarked coolly.

Unable to respond, I stood dumbfounded, watching him say a quick, private goodbye to the Smits. Poor Celia clung to him crying.

"Stefan, don't go," she pleaded. "Please."

He knelt down and gently placed both hands on each of her arms. "Dearest, I must go." Stefan glanced up at me. "I'm sure Lady Grace will take good care of you while I'm away, and I promise to write as often as I'm able."

Celia's lip quivered, and he gave her another quick hug.

"Have you said goodbye to your father?" I abruptly inquired.

"I'll be stopping by the hospital to do so on my way." Stefan put on his hat, tugged his uniform into place, and smiled at all of us in one sweeping glance as he swung his duffle bag over his shoulder. "Well, then I'll be on my way. The taxi is waiting."

"Let me walk you to the door," I offered, keeping my eyes away from Florence's disapproval. Stefan allowed me the honor to escort him, but Celia tagged along behind us.

"I'm coming too," she insisted.

Slightly irritated she had taken from me the privacy I needed, I could only express my anguish through a whisper.

"Why now?"

"It is better this way," he replied. "If I stay, you know it will only lead to heartache." Seemingly uncomfortable as Celia watched our conversation, he looked at her. "Sweetheart, go outside and tell the cabby I'll be right there."

"Okay."

Stefan pulled an envelope out of his pocket. "This is for you, Grace. Read it after I'm gone." He looked at me affectionately while my lower lip trembled. "Goodbye sweet Grace."

Immediately he stepped outdoors and gave Celia one last hug. As I watched from the open doorway, my heart broke. Closing my eyes, I couldn't bear to see another man leave for war. I listened as the car door opened, closed, and the tires crunch the pebbles underneath its tires as it drove away. The next I knew, Celia had run toward me, throwing her arms around my waist.

"I don't want him to die," she blubbered, heaving up and down in frightful tears.

"Neither do I, darling." Kneeling down before her, I held her tenderly. "Look at me, Celia." She wiped her nose with her sleeve and then brought her eyes to meet mine. "Every day you and I will say a prayer for your brother that God will keep him safe."

"Will God hear us?" she innocently asked.

"I hope so, dearest," I replied. "I hope so." We clung to each other for a few more minutes.

"Why don't you find Mrs. Smit and ask her to take you to the kitchen for a sweet snack?"

"Okay. I could use something sweet to feel better," she said, trying to smile.

As Celia ran down the hall, I returned upstairs to my room and closed the door behind me. My hands trembled clutching the envelope and breaking the seal.

"Dearest Grace. Forgive me for my abrupt departure. I think we both know that should I remain any longer at Stratton Park, we would partake in an affair with no positive outcome. As I leave you behind, be assured that you have captured my soul. If I could, I would marry you and never let you go. Providence, however, has not given us that gift. I shall, my love, carry you in my heart forever and cherish the memory of our night together. Love, Stefan."

How brutally right his words were to my wounded heart. As much as I hated to admit it, the man I had fallen in love with would never be mine. Instead, my heart had to return to Benedict, but I refused for Celia's sake and my sanity to stop praying that Stefan would survive the war.

Nervous Florence might find the penned note, I read it repeatedly until I had memorized his words. Afterward, I took a match by the fireplace, lit it at the corners, and tossed it into the hearth. As the paper burned and the words disappeared into unrecognizable ashes, I whispered, "I love you, Stefan."

CHAPTER 18

UNEXPECTED TIDINGS

As the weeks passed, letters arrived from both Benedict and Stefan. I felt torn between two men—the one I had vowed my life to in matrimony and the other I had given my heart in love. Stefan corresponded through his father and to Celia, who in turn reported to us he had been on the western front at Yser. Benedict, on the other hand, remained in France. His letters were less frequent, and I couldn't help but wonder if he were punishing me for my poorly hidden sentiments about Stefan. Florence had written and told him the lieutenant had returned to the front lines. No doubt he felt relieved my temptation had departed.

To fill the void I felt, I spent most of my time at Stratton Park with Celia, making sure she kept active. At the insistence of her father, he hired a private tutor to visit three times a week to return her to the routine of schooling. Celia balked at the notion, but I encouraged her to be obedient and do her best, as most young ladies did not have the opportunities for education.

Thankfully, Percy recovered from his cold, for which we were all grateful. The scare had reminded me to put my focus back on family and our son. Nevertheless, it did not completely repress the lingering affections for Stefan. Daydreaming about our night together had become a regular occurrence, especially in bed alone each night.

After two months had passed, I woke with morning queasiness. When my menses failed to arrive on schedule, it had become evident I had become pregnant. The closeness of my intimacy with Benedict and Stefan brought my state of mind into a panic. How would I ever know who had fathered the child? The guilt of my misdeed, no matter how wonderful it had been, brought dread to my heart.

Before writing to Benedict with the news or even suggesting to Florence I might be with child, I waited until the third month of my missed menses. With the continued physical symptoms and the rounding of my belly, I didn't need our practitioner's confirmation. Unable to express my condition to anyone, I sought out my only friend in Olivia.

Thankfully, she gradually recovered from the loss of Thomas but remained with her parents. Upon my arrival, she revealed shocking news that added to my fretfulness.

"I'm getting married again."

"What?" My mouth gaped open in shock.

"My parents arranged an amicable marriage with a fine gentleman named Gerard Killingworth. He is the elder son of a viscount who will inherit his title and lands. My parents find him and his family acceptable, of course."

"But Olivia, are you ready so soon after Thomas's death to engage your affections with another man?"

"He's a fine fellow, and I have no qualms about marrying him. Although, my affections are far less passionate than they were with Thomas." She lowered her eyes, appearing embarrassed over her confession.

"I hope you know what you're doing." I frowned with skepticism. "You've experienced true love once before, and I wouldn't think you would settle for anything less than it the second time."

"If I've learned anything," she said with a firm jaw, "it's that true love can bring more pain than it's worth. At least my parents will be pleased with the match, and my acceptance of their suggestions has healed our relationship."

"I see." Resigning myself to her choices, I despaired telling her my news. As I ruminated inwardly, my crinkled brow showed my distress. Olivia noticed it straight away.

"How are things with you?"

"I'm pregnant." The words flew from my lips as if I needed to confess my sin that I had been holding inside for months. Had she been a priest, I would have asked for absolution.

"How wonderful, Grace." In her exuberance, she gave me a quick embrace. "Benedict must be so happy."

Benedict. My poor husband, wandering the trenches in France and experiencing hell. Suddenly I felt awful for not writing, thinking the delightful news might give him hope.

"I've not told him yet." My lower lip quivered. Of course, the truth of the matter prevented my confession. "I'm not sure if he or Stefan is the father of the child."

Olivia brought her hand to her mouth to stifle a gasp. "Oh, dear Lord in heaven," she exclaimed. "You mean you . . ." Her words trailed off as if she were waiting for me to finish the sentence.

"After our conversation of last, I went to him. You told me to grab whatever I could for a few moments of joy, and I did." The appalling shock on her face surprised me. I felt cheeky to have blamed my actions because of her advice.

"It appears my mourning had encouraged

you far too well," she replied, nervously clutching her hands together. "I cannot help but feel somewhat responsible."

"You have no responsibility whatsoever for my choices," I swiftly assured her. "I fell in love with him and he with me. It just happened."

"Have you told him you are pregnant?"

"No, he left immediately afterward and returned to his regiment."

"Oh, Grace, I'm so sorry. What will you do?"

"Have the baby and raise it as Benedict's child. What else can I do?"

"What a dreadful state of affairs," she groaned. Olivia wrapped her arm around my shoulder.

"I'm beginning to show, so I need to tell Florence and write to Benedict."

"Will you tell Stefan?"

"No." I sighed. "I dare not write him directly through his father, but no doubt he'll discover it soon enough when the news is announced."

"Perhaps Benedict will come home from the front," she said in an encouraging tone.

"I doubt it. He's too patriotic to ask for another leave when fighting needs to be done." As I finished my words, a wave of nausea swept through my body, reminding me further of my condition. The joy I should have felt upon having another child felt doused with distress. For my sanity, I needed to focus on the future.

"Will you invite me to the wedding?" I purposely asked, wishing to take my mind elsewhere.

"More than that," Olivia said, flashing a broad smile. "Will you be my matron of honor?"

Faced with the realization I would witness her second marriage to someone she did not love, I hesitated. "Oh, Olivia, tell me you are not making a mistake." She lowered her head and sat motionless for a few minutes.

"I have no worries that he, too, will be sent overseas as he was unable to serve due to chronic asthma. At least I need not fear he will die anytime soon and break my heart."

"Still . . ." My lips pursed in disagreement. "You don't love him."

"He's a fine enough fellow," Olivia half-heartedly replied. "I'm sure that he will treat me with respect. Then perhaps I will have a baby too."

Naturally, I couldn't deny Olivia should enjoy motherhood, having remembered she and Thomas were unable to succeed. Even if her new marriage would not compare to the relationship with her deceased husband, at least she would have comfort in children.

"Then I would be honored."

"Thank you, my dear friend." Olivia gave me

a tight hug.

"Girls, would you like some tea and cake?" Olivia's mother stood in the parlor threshold, smiling at us.

"That would be nice, Mother," Olivia replied. "Grace has agreed to be my matron of honor."

"Splendid!"

"I hope you've chosen Olivia a kind gentleman who will cherish and love her," I said, giving her mother a subtle hint of disapproval in my gaze.

"Stop worrying about me." Olivia scolded me in return. "I'll be fine."

For her sake, I despised the notion she settled because of her brokenness over losing Thomas. My hand rested gently on my belly, reminding me of my future. I would bear a son or daughter who might never know who had fathered their life.

The following morning as I sat at the breakfast table, I felt extremely ill. Doctor Reyer had joined us for the meal. Florence sat sipping her tea and reading the paper while Celia rattled like a chatterbox at her father, attempting to gain as much attention as possible.

After spooning a few scrambled eggs upon

my plate, I passed by the remaining food selections. When I sat down, I took a piece of dry toast and left the butter and marmalade far from my reach. My actions immediately piqued Martin's attention.

"No appetite this morning?"

"I'm afraid not." Not quite ready to explain the reason why I ignored his inquiry, I turned my attention to Celia, who had decided to focus on her food. As I considered doing something with her wild hair again, Doctor Reyer interrupted my thoughts.

"Stefan has managed to write." He pulled out an envelope from the inside pocket of his waistcoat. "By the look of its condition, I'm surprised it made it to England." The paper looked dirty and tattered as if it had been drenched by the muddy fields of the front lines.

"Good news, I hope." Without thought, the words flew from between my lips, and with uncontrolled excitement, I perked up like a wilted flower. Everyone noticed, including Florence, who disapprovingly pulled her mouth to one side.

"As good as can be expected," he somberly replied. "He remains unharmed, and for that I am grateful."

"What else does he say, Papa?" Celia attempted to snatch the envelope, but her father pulled it away from her grasp.

"He sends his love to you Celia and best wishes to the Smits and the rest of the household."

The *rest of the household*. My heart sank. What did I expect him to say—send my love to Grace? The mentioning of his name and the knowledge of his whereabouts inflamed my emotions to an uncontrollable moan.

"Excuse me," I abruptly announced. In a quick movement, I rose and pushed the chair out from underneath me. "I'm not well." Doctor Reyer stood to his feet and halted my step with a soft touch upon my forearm.

"Is there something that I can do?"

"What is it, Grace? If you are ill, let Martin tend to you," Florence ordered.

Nervously I glanced at my mother-in-law, Celia, and then saw the Smits heading in our direction to join us for breakfast. As I considered the opportunity, I decided to take up his offer.

"Might we talk in private, Doctor Reyer? Perhaps in my husband's study."

"Yes, of course." He nodded at Florence. "If you would excuse me for a moment, Lady Russell."

With a quick step, I headed down the hall as Martin followed me. Once inside, I hastily shut the door. A terrible urge to blurt out my dilemma tingled on my tongue. His brow furrowed, showing his concern as the seconds ticked to the tune of the clock on the mantel. At last I uttered the words.

"I believe I'm pregnant, Doctor Reyer."

He stared at me wide-eyed. "And why do you think you are pregnant?" he asked. "What are your symptoms?"

"I've missed my menses for three months," I shyly admitted. "The morning nausea, as you can see, has plagued me for the past month." When I lowered my head and placed my hands on my abdomen, I indicated the obvious. "My belly, I'm afraid, is beginning to round."

"Well then, I agree you must be with child, but it's not my responsibility to examine you. I suggest, Lady Grace, you see your private medical professional regarding the matter." His demeanor became sullen and irritable. The atmosphere in the room grew tense as I stood before him, witnessing his accusatory stare. I responded in a defensive tone.

"Why do you look at me with such disregard?" My chest heaved. "You asked me my symptoms, and I have told you. My husband shall be elated we are having another child."

Without hesitation, he shot back, narrowing his eyes at me. "Are you sure it's your husband's or is it my son's?"

Overwhelmed by the accusation, I stumbled backward until I felt myself flush to a chair. "How dare you presume to suggest I am an adulteress?" Suddenly I felt trapped as his formidable demeanor stood before me. My face burned with embarrassment, signifying my guilt.

"I've been keenly aware of my son's regard for you and you for him," he continued. "The early-morning hours in which you awakened me to tend Percy had confirmed what I had suspected the evening before."

"Suspected what?" I asked as my body trembled.

"I had found the bright moonlight streaming into my bedroom that evening to be somewhat annoying and rose to close the draperies. When I glanced out the window, I saw you leave the manor. Naturally, I knew where your midnight walk would take you based on the direction you were heading."

"You know nothing." My continued denial felt as if I were burying myself alive in shovels of lies.

"I know full well, Lady Grace. Before I went to work, I confronted Stefan regarding the encounter between the two of you. The boy has never been able to lie to me straight to my face, so he admitted what had transpired. To save you both from further disgrace, I ordered him to leave posthaste since he was well enough to do so."

After finishing his startling announcement, I plopped down into a nearby chair. My legs lost their strength as I stood accused, judged, and found guilty by the testimony of my lover. Why had Stefan told his father? He had betrayed our secret and put me in grave danger of losing everything. Impulsively I buried my face in my hands.

"You have not told Lady Russell, have you?" My voice cracked in trepidation.

"No, it's not my position to expose your indiscretions. Since the child, I'm assuming, could very well be your husband's."

Sheepishly I lifted my head and saw he had softened his countenance to one of pity. "Thank you, Doctor Reyer."

He pulled out his pocket watch and noted the time. "If you will excuse me, I must take my leave to the hospital." He hesitated and then spoke in a harsh tone. "I shall not tell my son of your condition. The less he knows, the better."

As he left me alone, trembling in the chair in which I landed, I feared Florence would suspect the same scenario. Remembering she had inquired as to why I was dressed so early in the morning hours while standing in Percy's nursery, it could be plausible she might presume the child may not be Benedict's baby. My heart pounded in my chest as I considered the outcome of my announcement.

After deliberating about my state of affairs, I rose to my feet and proceeded to the dining room to find Florence, Celia, and the Smits finishing their breakfast. I returned to my seat and took a sip of my cold tea. Florence gave me no rest and immediately questioned me.

"What did Martin say?"

Setting my teacup down with a clank onto the saucer, I lifted my eyes and announced, "He agrees with my assessment that I am undoubtedly three months pregnant."

Florence gasped, and a broad grin spread across her face.

"You're going to have a baby?" Celia squealed.

"Yes, a baby," I responded, "which my dear husband hoped for when he came to visit us a few months ago."

"Hearty congratulations," Mr. Smit offered. Gretta grinned. "Oh, indeed. What pleasing news!"

As everyone gave congratulatory praises, I looked at Florence and forced a half smile.

"You must write straightaway to Benedict and tell him the news," she insisted. Florence patted my hand lying limply by my teacup and gave it a quick squeeze of approval. "I am most pleased, Grace. Percy will have a sibling to enjoy."

"Yes, he will," I replied, wondering what it would be like to have a son nearly three and a crying baby in our midst. The joys of motherhood remained aloof. In fact, to my shame, I dreaded giving birth.

On the surface, Florence showed no signs of thinking the baby could be anyone else's except Benedict's, and for that small gift I remained thankful. As long as Doctor Reyer kept his promise to remain silent, my secret would be safe.

CHAPTER 19

PASSAGE OF TIME

England had entered the third year of the dreadful war that by now had taken the lives of millions worldwide. As I stood before the mirror in my ninth month of pregnancy, nothing of substance had changed except my burgeoning belly. Infrequent correspondence transpired between Martin and Stefan while Benedict announced he would soon return for a long overdue leave. As an officer, he had been entitled to a leave every three months but had forgone that privilege for some time. I thought his actions ill-advised, but his patriotism and determination to help win the war hindered him from doing otherwise.

Celia had been a great comfort to me in months past as we kept our promises to keep Stefan in prayer. Naturally, I made sure to pray for Benedict in the same breath, lest she question my reasons. In her childlike trust, she witnessed in me no ulterior motives nor did she suspect I carried anything but friendly concern for her brother. Doctor Reyer, on the other hand, had remained aloof toward me during my pregnancy, and we never spoke again of the affair.

Olivia had insisted I attend her wedding, which I did to honor her request, in spite of my pregnant state. It had been a small, private affair instead of a large, lavish church wedding. Outwardly she appeared happy enough with her newfound husband. Her parents, of course, were delighted with her change of heart. Nevertheless, a part of me remained sorrowful over the loss of Thomas and her latest decisions.

On the day of Benedict's arrival, I waited at home while our driver picked him up at the station. It had been a miserable pregnancy, and in the last weeks, my feet had swollen and my lower back ached with every movement. Florence and I invited the staff to stand out of doors to welcome his long overdue visit. Nervously I waited alongside his mother and watched the motorcar approach and come to a halt. The chauffeur opened the door. Benedict's boots slowly met the pebbled driveway, but with his hat and head bowed downward, I could not see his face. His movements appeared labored until gradually Benedict adjusted his posture and stood upright.

Nothing could have prepared me for what I witnessed. Compared to his first leave, Benedict looked in his sixties. The few strands of gray in his temples had blended into a noticeable white patch. Deep lines etched his forehead, and his eyebrows furrowed together as if they were positioned in a permanent frown. Benedict expressed no joy or pleasure when he glanced at his mother and me, his lips pressed in a straight line. Heartbroken at the sight of him, I stepped forward and greeted him with a soft kiss on his right cheek. He tilted his head away, avoiding a prolonged show of affection.

"Benedict, darling, welcome home." His eyes scanned the staff standing at attention, and he flashed a noticeable scowl.

"Dismiss them," he commanded under his breath.

Shocked at his attitude, I stepped away. He walked past me and headed for his mother. As he stood talking to her, I glanced at Carter who appeared as confused as I had been at my husband's actions.

"You may thank the staff, but I think it is best they return to their duties."

"Yes, my lady."

Carter nodded at me and quietly dismissed everyone while I returned to Benedict's side. He had already taken his mother's arm and stepped through the threshold into the foyer. When Benedict halted, an air of irritation swirled in the atmosphere.

"I am exhausted, so if you'll excuse me, I'm going to retire." His shoulders drooped in a defeated manner, and I glanced at Florence, whose face displayed the same concern as my own.

"Let me at least walk with you to the bedchamber," I offered. Surprised he didn't protest, I climbed the stairs alongside him. He clutched the railing the entire way to the top and then halted after hearing me pant from being out of breath. It felt as if I were carrying a ten-pound sack of potatoes around my waist with each step.

"I'm sorry, Grace, I should have given you my arm." His eyes lowered to my abdomen as his hand touched my rounded belly. "Boy or girl, you think?"

"Girl," I quickly announced. "If it were a boy, I'd probably be carrying the load a bit lower. At least that is your mother's wise conclusion."

"Yes, I can see you are carrying this baby higher than you did Percy." A small grin curled the corner of his lips. When our eyes met, his gaze appeared empty as if his soul had departed. I knew then the war had taken its toll in more ways than I could imagine.

"Why don't you go to our room, get undressed, and climb into bed," I suggested. "You look weary, Benedict."

"I intend to," he said. "Peace and quiet is what I crave."

"I understand." Purposely, I did not follow him as he opened the door to our bedroom suite and disappeared. A myriad of emotions stirred inwardly, resurrecting thoughts of Stefan still on the front lines. What, if anything, had it done to him by now, being back in the thick of fighting?

Filled with distress, I went downstairs and found Florence in the parlor staring out the window. After hearing me enter, she turned around. Her hands clutched together in a worrisome manner.

"Something is terribly wrong," she blurted. "Benedict is not well."

Sharing her concern, I agreed. "He appears exhausted not only physically but mentally." My back ached, and I swiftly sat down to ease the discomfort. "Perhaps whatever rest we can give him while on leave will help restore him before he returns."

"I do hope so," Florence replied. "Honestly, I wish he would never return."

While Florence was talking, the baby gave me a good kick. "Oh dear," I moaned. "This child is anxious to be free of my womb." My hand rubbed over the spot where the baby had announced its presence, causing me to smile. I thought perhaps I would have at least another week or two before birth, but a second later my water broke, gushing between my legs.

"Oh dear God in heaven." I squealed. "Florence!" Seeping through my dress and running down my legs, the mortification snatched the breath from my lungs. Florence moved to my side and bellowed at the top of her voice for Carter. He entered the room in a tizzy, took one look at me, the puddle on the floor, and gasped.

"I'll call the physician immediately," he blurted in horror.

"Oh, Florence, this is too soon. I wanted Benedict to rest." I groaned, feeling the first pangs of labor.

"Come along now," she calmly cajoled. "We'll put you in my bedroom to birth the baby and let him sleep through it all if he can."

"You expect me not to scream when this child rips me apart?" I asked, struggling to stand on my feet. Already I felt like shouting at the top of my lungs for the inopportune moment the baby had chosen to arrive.

"You'll do just fine." Florence comforted me.

Nothing would be all right. Childbirth could never be a pleasant occurrence and was always fraught with the possibility of terrible outcomes for the mother and baby. Desperately I needed the comfort of a man and my husband's reassurance, but once again, Benedict could not satisfy my need.

After a thankful short five hours of labor, my body finally released the child within. A little girl came into the world, screaming and crying with a shrill tone. When I had the opportunity to hold her in my arms, she was tiny compared to Percy, who had been a hefty boy at birth. The ruddy-faced girl who cried with her eyes closed felt like a soft feather pillow.

"She so small." Concerned, I glanced up at our family practitioner, Doctor Radcliffe.

"Yes, she's a bit underweight."

Florence, who like an angel had been with me throughout my ordeal, gave me an encouraging smile. "Benedict will be so pleased."

Benedict. I had barely thought about him during the delivery, and a pang of guilt stabbed my heart.

"Is he all right?"

"Yes, he's waiting in the hall."

Nanny Jane took the baby from my arms. "Let me clean her up," she said. "Doctor Radcliffe wants to take a look at her."

"Yes, of course." I watched as he listened to her heart, checked every finger and toe, and apparently seemed pleased at her health. Nanny Jane helped clean up the afterbirth and bloodied sheets. Florence didn't appear to care I had given birth in her bed because I knew she had given birth to Benedict in the same room over forty years ago.

Their fussing over me ended, and the baby came back into my arms. With love, I observed the adorable, swaddled girl. She had stopped screaming and peered up at me with brilliant blue eyes. Blond tufts of hair made her look like a porcelain doll. The babe held none of my dark-haired features or those of Benedict's, and I feared he would notice.

"Let me go get him." Florence said, seemingly unaffected by her granddaughter's features.

"I wouldn't worry about her size," Doctor Radcliffe said. "She's small but seems hearty enough. Keep her warm and well fed, and I'm sure she'll put on weight soon."

A few minutes later, Benedict entered the room with Florence. He ambled to the side of my bed and gazed down at the baby.

"We have a daughter. Would you like to hold her?" Waiting for him to respond, he merely stared at her with a blank expression on his face. He showed no emotion of joy at her arrival or aversion either. When he wouldn't take her, I hugged her tightly to my breast.

"She's tiny," he somberly remarked.

"Yes, compared to Percy, she is a few pounds lighter."

Suddenly Florence spoke as she came to stand by Benedict's side. "She has my mother's eyes and complexion. Even her little button nose."

"Your mother was Swedish, was she not?" I asked her, hoping to reiterate the likeness.

"Yes, from Stockholm."

"Then I am happy she carries your family traits." Naturally, I would never really know if her fairness was due to Stefan's genes or that of Florence's mother. Nevertheless, the baby had arrived. "What shall we name her?" I asked. Benedict did not respond as he continued to stare at the baby. Turning to Florence, I asked. "Wasn't your mother's name Amelia?"

"Yes." Her eyes brightened with a hopeful glint.

"Then I would like to name her Amelia Florence." Looking up at Benedict, I entreated his agreement. "What do you think, darling?"

Suddenly the baby started to wail in my arms. Benedict stepped back and scowled. Her shrill voice caused him to bring his hands to his ears, and he shook his head.

"Make her stop that noise," he pleaded.

"Honey, she's a baby," I cajoled him. "She's going to cry." My reasoning had no effect upon Benedict. He spun around, pushed past Florence, and left the room. Shocked at his outburst, Florence gawked at his behavior.

"I'll go tend to him." She sighed.

When she left, I spoke to Doctor Radcliffe, who was closing his bag and preparing to leave.

"Something is wrong with him," I cried. "He hasn't been himself since he came home from France earlier today."

"When was the last time the baron had taken a leave?"

"At least nine months," I answered, glancing down at the baby making a gesture.

He shook his head. "We've been seeing many men in the hospital who are returning with multiple symptoms. Depression, anxiety, sensitivity to loud noises. My peers and I agree it is some type of battle fatigue after being on the front lines for prolonged periods."

Troubled that Benedict suffered this malady, I pointedly asked, "Tell me what I can do for him?"

"Rest. He needs quiet too."

Considering my darling little girl in my

arms, I didn't want Benedict to go back to war. What I wanted was this war to be over and another chance to make things right in my marriage.

"Let me take her now." Nanny Jane came to my bedside. "You need rest too, my lady."

The fatigue of childbirth swiftly engulfed me, and I felt utterly drained.

"I agree," Doctor Radcliffe firmly stated. "It's time for you to do the same."

When they left the room and closed the door, I promptly fell asleep.

Chapter 20

No Peace

By the end of the week, it became evident something terribly evil plagued my husband. The slightest loud noise caused him to jump. He woke me up multiple times in the night with night terrors, screaming in a chilling roar. Each time, it took me at least an hour to comfort him before he could sleep again.

When I tried to display any affection such as a simple kiss, he spurned my actions. During the day, instead of bonding with his son or paying attention to the baby, he remained detached. For hours he would hide in his study for solitude, giving Carter orders to keep his decanter full of brandy.

Florence begged Doctor Reyer to spend some time with Benedict alone to ascertain his state of mind. One evening during dinner drinks, he took the opportunity. It appeared to be a short conversation, because ten minutes afterward, Benedict stormed down the hallway to his study and slammed the door.

Martin and Hugo joined us in the parlor later, and I could tell by the look on their faces the news would not be good. Doctor Reyer sat down and with a somber face gave his opinion.

"The baron definitely suffers from a severe case of battle fatigue. If I were you, I would recommend he not return to France. His regiment commander should be directly apprised of his condition."

"It's terribly alarming," Hugo interjected. "I felt sorry for the man."

"What can be done?" Florence asked.

"To be frank, he needs to be hospitalized."

"Hospitalized?" I balked. The thought sent shivers through my veins. "Are you suggesting my husband should be placed in an asylum?"

"I won't hear of it!" Florence recoiled in horror. "Surely being home with his family for another two weeks will help alleviate his tension."

Doctor Reyer shook his head negatively. "I wouldn't count on a mere two weeks, Lady Russell. These recoveries, under the right medical supervision, can take months if not years. I'm finding many of these soldiers end up discharged as a result of their inability to return to duty."

"I'm sorry, but I think it's too early in Benedict's return to jump to any conclusions as to what should be done," I replied in a tone of respect instead of the seething anger flowing in my veins. "I agree with Florence that such drastic measures are out of the question. He needs family, rest, and to be around those who love him. I cannot under any circumstances relegate my husband to a mental hospital."

Florence nodded her head in agreement, showing she approved of my edict.

"If you feel that strongly, then I shall not interfere. However, I would at least make it a point to write to his commanding officer and ask for an extension of his leave if anything."

"We can agree to that course of action," Florence replied. "Don't you think that's wise, Grace?"

"Yes, absolutely. I'd rather he not return at all if I had my way." Concerned that Benedict had stormed off to be alone, I rose to my feet. "If you will excuse me," I announced. "I'm going to check on my husband."

As I strode down the hallway to his study, I stubbornly refused to believe he needed anything except rest and love. When I reached the door, I softly knocked and opened it a crack.

"May I come in?" My head peeked around the doorframe.

"If you wish," he responded in a monotone fashion.

Slowly I walked up to his desk and sat down

in a chair facing him. He had a glass of brandy, which he picked up and brought to his lips. It broke my heart to see his hand trembling as he did so.

"You've been drinking a lot since you came home," I calmly remarked. "Do you think that is wise?"

His eyes narrowed at me, and he slammed the glass down on the desktop. "I don't give a damn if it's wise of not. It settles my nerves."

My arrival had disturbed his moment alone, and I questioned whether I should have come to speak with him. Having expressed his irritable mood, I kept my voice calm and affectionate.

"Percy misses you. He's been asking for his daddy, and the baby . . ." As I spoke, I could see the irritation in his eyes increase.

"I can't handle it right now, Grace. A bothersome child, a crying baby, and that damn Belgian girl running our hallways, yelling at the top of her lungs. I came home for peace, damn it!"

My heart broke watching his face contort into a menacing sneer. Softly I whispered to him with pleading eyes. "What has happened to my dear husband?"

He stared at me for some time as if I were daft. Perhaps I should have known what had happened, what horrors he had seen, what atrocities, noise, and death had surrounded him for months on end. However, my life had been far from the reality of the trenches as I lived safely in our home every day while he gave his life to protect it.

His hand fiddled with the glass on the top of his desk for a few moments. He lifted his eyes and spoke.

"You want to know what happens on the battlefield, Grace? I'll tell you." He leaned forward on the desktop and stared intently into my eyes. "Bombs explode around you, blowing up the landscape along with soldiers and horses. Afterward, your ears ring and you go partially deaf when one explodes a few yards away, and you're lucky enough to survive the flying shrapnel. Others who were too close have their legs and arms ripped off or their faces disfigured. Germans with machine guns riddle young boys with bullet holes, leaving them dead or dying a slow death in agony lying in the mud. I ordered them to advance in the line of fire. I've killed Germans, plenty of Germans, some begging for my mercy, and I gladly murdered them anyway. The mud, rain, and heat of the summer changes to the cold and snow in the winter. Boys lucky enough to dodge bullets die from dysentery instead. The stench of rotting corpses and human waste fills the air." His eyes grew wide with rage. "And the worst part? It goes on and on, battles for hours, with no reprieve. And all we have gained is a few centimeters into the enemy's territory."

"Oh dear God," I groaned. The sights and smells he described overwhelmed me.

"It's hell, Grace! It's hell on earth!"

Benedict's voice boomed at me, causing me to flinch. In all our years together, I had no reason to fear Benedict, but in his eyes, I saw a disturbing glint of insanity.

"Please, darling, don't go back," I pleaded with a trembling voice. "Tell your commanding officer you are ill and cannot return."

"They will brand me a coward," he grimly replied.

"Then get medical help."

"My ancestors will think me a weakling."

"Your ancestors?" I spat. Instantly I hated every picture of his descendants that hung in the estate. It was an argument he always brought up. Centuries of brave men who fought Napoleon or wherever else the British Empire found conflict. "Yes, I know your ancestors were all military men, but they are dead, Benedict. You have nothing to prove to anyone and a family who cares and loves you. There is no shame in getting help."

"You sound like that damn surgeon whatever his name is," he snarled.

Suddenly I felt helpless. My pleas fell on deaf

ears and a proud heart, albeit a wounded one.

"If you insist on returning, then rest," I pleaded. "Please rest while you are here."

"I can't. Everything in this household irritates me to no end. The children, my mother, the servants scurrying around, even Carter and his booming voice. I despise the man."

"And me?" He had purposely left me out of his list of irritations, but I knew I fit in there somewhere.

"Leave me alone, Grace. Go back and tend to the children."

As I gazed at him staring into his empty glass, the urge to shake him by the shoulders tempted me. Embarrassed at my lack of tolerance and understanding for his disorder, I pondered what, if anything, I could do to help. There would be no quiet in the household, but I didn't wish him placed in a hospital either. Then I remembered the one location of peace on the estate.

"Go to the hunting cottage and stay there, Benedict. No one will bother you. It will be peaceful, and you can sleep and relax to your heart's content." It was a valid suggestion, and I thought it a good plan. "You can take walks, enjoy the wildlife, smell the clean, fresh air, and take the time to forget the horrors of war."

He lifted his head and gave me an agreeable nod. "I would like that," he responded.

"Wonderful." I rose to my feet. "I'll tell the housekeeper to ready the cottage for your stay in the morning." A burden lifted from my shoulders, knowing I had thought of another plan to help him recuperate while at home.

His sudden change of heart encouraged me. For a brief second I noticed a slight grin brighten his face. Perhaps I had found the answer to his current dilemma.

The following morning, I accompanied Benedict to the cottage. We loaded the car with everything we thought he would need and added a few books for his reading enjoyment. When I arrived, I desperately tried to push away the memories of my illicit affair with Stefan. It wasn't the time to think about the past or to wallow in my regrets. Instead, my husband needed me, and I focused on him and our new baby.

As the driver helped to unload the car, I accompanied Benedict inside. My husband did not bring up the subject of Stefan's former occupancy, so neither did I.

"I had forgotten this cottage altogether," he remarked. He glanced around at the furnishings, walked to the bedroom, and returned to look out the front window, shaded by the overhang of the porch. The days were getting cooler, so I knew the interior would be comfortable.

"There are plenty of blankets in the closet and extra pillows if you need them," I announced. "Carter has stocked wood for the fireplace in case you need to take off the chill." When the driver brought in the basket of food from the kitchen, he came to my side to look at its contents. "You will join us for dinner each evening, won't you? I'll have the chauffeur pick you up at seven if that's convenient."

"I'll eat here," he replied in a sullen tone. "I don't wish to be with people right now."

Hurt he had decided to forgo time with the family, I took his hand in mine. His brow furrowed over my touch, and he looked into my eyes.

"May I stay with you this evening?"

"Why?"

"To comfort you, Benedict."

He shook his head negatively and pulled his hand from mine. "I want to be on my own."

Disappointed at his spurning remarks, I wanted to leave straightaway. I glanced around and noticed all the supplies we had brought were inside. He had walked over to the window and stared at the landscape. Without asking for permission, I put my arms around him and gave him a lingering hug. He stood rigid and unmoving. Helpless that I could not reach him in any fashion, I relinquished my hold and walked to the door.

"I love you, darling. Get rest, and I'll come back and check on you in the morning." He did not appear to welcome another visit and flashed a disagreeable glare in my direction. "Well, perhaps not tomorrow," I said, correcting my plans. "I will be back in a few days."

After saying my goodbyes, I climbed back in the car. For the first time in my life, I bit my nails on my right hand. I felt utterly powerless to help him and terrified for the future.

CHAPTER 21

CASUALTY OF WAR

Benedict had cloistered himself at the cottage for days on end, refusing to eat evening meals at the estate. He barked at the housemaid assigned to tend to his needs, demanding solitude. Carter received orders Benedict didn't wish visits from either his mother or me, for that matter. Even though we felt hurt and discarded, Florence and I discussed it would be best if we left Benedict alone in the hopes that soon he would recuperate before his return to duty.

We were able to convince Martin to check on him, but his visit was unwelcome and agitated Benedict more than helped. Upon Doctor Reyer's return, he reiterated his concern about Benedict's well-being, continuing to suggest we have him hospitalized. Florence maintained her aversion to the idea, believing we were the ones that could help. I, on the other hand, began to fret that perhaps we were making a mistake. The days were swiftly slipping by and drawing closer to

Benedict's return to France.

Florence and I had written Benedict's commanding officer, as suggested by Martin, to extend his leave. Unfortunately, we had not received a response. Two days before he was due to travel back to his regiment, I instructed Carter to check my husband's welfare and see if there was anything he needed to prepare for the return. At least he had allowed our butler the opportunity to visit and replenish his food supplies if nothing else.

While Carter performed his duties, Florence had been downstairs reading in the parlor, while I had just finished nursing Amelia in the nursery. Our daughter showed signs of strengthening and growth each day, and I felt assured she would develop into a beautiful little girl. Poor Percy had felt slighted by his father's abandonment, but Nanny Jane kept him occupied in other childish pursuits.

As I lay Amelia down in her bassinet for a nap, I lifted my head to see Carter standing in the doorway.

"Might I have a word, Lady Grace" He somberly spoke.

The tone of his voice alarmed me along with his troubled countenance. He fidgeted with his hands and took deep breaths.

"Yes, of course." We stepped out into the

hallway, and Carter, in an out-of-character move, took my hand.

"My lady, there is no easy way to tell you."

"Tell me what?" My heart raced in my chest.

"The baron . . ." His voice choked.

"Carter, what is it?" I demanded.

"I'm afraid, my lady, that the baron is dead."

The word echoed through my mind as if it bounced off the walls of a cavern—*dead, dead, dead.*

"Whatever do you mean?" I cried. My hand crushed his in return.

"I can barely say the words." Carter halted and then answered in a raspy voice. "He used . . . he used his service revolver to take his life."

Everything around me disappeared except Carter's face. His eyes watered, and his trembling voice told me he had spoken the truth. Paralyzed at the thought of Benedict's act of desperation, I stood stunned, unable to move. My heart beat thunderously in my chest until I wailed aloud, "Oh dear God, no."

Tears should have run down my cheeks from sorrow, but instead, I felt as if the angel of death had thrust a knife into my chest. The horror incapacitated my ability to cry. It wasn't supposed to end this way.

"Why, Carter? Why did he do such a thing?" My shock demanded answers.

"Perhaps he could not face returning, your ladyship." He handed me a piece of paper. "The baron left this behind."

Snatching it from Carter's hand, I read the words written by Benedict's apparent trembling pen. *"Forgive me. I'd be branded a coward if I stayed and would become a coward if I returned."*

In my wildest imaginations, I had never believed Benedict would do such a ghastly thing no matter how disturbed he had been from the war. He chose to die instead of seek treatment. The other alternative of returning to the front he could not face. Death had lured him to take its final path as the only way to peace.

"Have you told Lady Russell?" I sputtered.

"Not yet. I thought it best I speak to you first."

"Is his body still at the cottage," I asked, cringing at the unseen sight.

"Yes, my lady. He's lying on the bed, and I've covered him."

"I want to see him." My hand pulled from Carter, but he stopped me by grabbing my upper arm and shaking his head no.

"I don't think that's wise, your ladyship. It's not something a woman of your stature should look at, my lady. The baron wouldn't want you to remember him in such a terrible physical state."

The baron hadn't given thought to what he

had done and how he had just destroyed his life and ours with one single bullet.

"All right then," I agreed. "I must tell his mother. Come with me, Carter. I cannot do this alone."

We slowly walked downstairs and strode to the parlor door as if I had already begun the funeral walk behind Benedict's coffin. Florence sat sipping a cup of tea, her latest book lay in her lap, and she appeared content. When she lifted her eyes and saw us together in the doorway, she smiled at first. Neither of us spoke, and as the silence continued, her smile faded.

"What is it?"

After swallowing the lump in my throat, I entered and sat down next to her on the divan. "Oh, Florence," I whispered. A tear welled in my eye and trickled down my cheek. My paralyzed emotions released when I spoke his name. "It's Benedict."

"What about Benedict?" She glanced back and forth at us. I lifted my eyes to Carter, pleading for him to say the words.

"I'm afraid, Lady Russell, that the baron is dead."

She gasped and brought her hand to her mouth. "Dead? What on earth do you mean?" She grabbed me by the arm. "Tell me, Grace. What does he mean?"

With quivering lips, I relayed the painful truth. "Benedict was far worse than we believed, Florence. He shot himself with his service revolver." After I had spoken the words, I sobbed. Florence dropped her cup and saucer to the floor, shattering it at our feet as our lives had at that moment.

Apprehensive that Florence would have a spell, I pulled her into my arms, and we both cried together. When I could speak again, I rose from the divan and walked over to Carter.

"You will need to call the constable, Carter. Since there is a weapon involved, I'm sure they will want to examine the scene and his body."

"Yes, your ladyship. Right away."

Carter turned to leave, but when he did so, poor Florence tried to rise to her feet. She beheld me with tearful eyes, and a moment later, fainted, slumping onto the floor. I ran to her side and knelt down.

"Carter, call Doctor Reyer at the hospital, and have him come home posthaste."

"Yes, my lady. Right away."

Florence's eyelids fluttered, and she moaned. Conscious, her anguish returned.

"Oh, Benedict, Benedict, what have you done?" she cried.

For some time, I cradled Florence in my arms, waiting for Martin and the onslaught of police. The days ahead would not be easy. The investigation, the inquest, and the ruling of Benedict taking his life would take its toll upon us all. With Doctor Reyer's testimony and that of his wife and mother, inevitably the authorities would conclude he took his life while in a state of unsound mind.

At that moment, I knew Benedict had been a casualty of war like the others who fell in the midst of a battle on foreign soil. He had suffered a different kind of fatal wound—one of the mind instead of the flesh. I knew then I had loved him after all.

CHAPTER 22

PEACE AT LAST

When armistice arrived, everything changed again. Before the war, my life had been like a picture puzzle. All the pieces fit together in one idyllic scene. In a cruel twist of fate, war arrived and twisted everything upside down. As it raged worldwide and years passed, the pieces found their way back together. By the end, it had created an entirely different image with a lost piece in the middle— my husband.

We buried Benedict in the family plot at Stratton Park next to his father. Laden with guilt and depression, the tables had spun on me. Olivia became my confidante and comfort through sorrow as I had once been to her. Florence grieved with the support of Doctor Reyer, and over the past year, their relationship had grown closer. I had been of little help in that regard, struggling with my newfound life of being a single mother.

Percy, now four years old and robbed of a

father, remained healthy. It saddened me he would never know his father who loved him dearly. Nevertheless, as his only son, he would inherit Benedict's title and estate, and I would be responsible for helping him receive that inheritance with education and wisdom. Amelia turned one year of age as a beautiful blond little girl, and to my surprise took on Benedict's characteristics as well as her grandmother's every day. Though a year ago I had concerns the child would be Stefan's, I now felt relieved to have given Benedict another baby as he desired.

My affair with Stefan faded into obscurity in my thoughts. It seemed like another lifetime that I had fallen in love with a young Belgian soldier. Perhaps I should have regretted my actions, but I absolved myself of my sin because Benedict had failed to fill that one void in my life, leaving me vulnerable. I forgave my husband and myself. Now the war had ended, it didn't matter any longer. Providence had taken my life in a different direction.

Almost immediately after armistice, the Smits returned home. As quickly as the refugees had arrived in England, a mass exodus to their homeland ensued with the same eagerness. Florence and I agreed their presence had been a wonderful gift in our household. Gretta was kind enough to leave some of her recipes with the cook after spoiling us for years.

Saying goodbye to Doctor Reyer and especially Celia had been the most difficult. Celia, now almost fourteen years of age, had blossomed into an incredible young lady. She had kept with her studies, and to her father's delight, showed herself to be a bright and astute student. If anyone had been anxious to return home, it had been her for the sheer joy of seeing her brother.

Stefan had survived by the grace of God and our many prayers. As I reflected on the past, I chided myself for not praying enough for Benedict. The guilt over his suicide hung heavily upon me as I blamed myself for sending him to the cottage and isolating him from those who loved and cared for his welfare. Nonetheless, I surmised Benedict's ancestral pride had played a factor in his inability to humble himself to get the aid he needed at Martin's suggestion.

Doctor Reyer reported Stefan had recently arrived at their home and happily found it still standing although it had been ransacked and damaged to some extent. He began the process of restoration as he waited for his family's return. Doctor Reyer planned to start another private practice and restore their lives to a semblance of normalcy.

As we stood in the foyer, stating our

goodbyes, I could see Florence struggle with her emotions. She bit her lower lip when Martin took both her hands into his.

"Lady Russell, what words can I express for your hospitality during these past years? Celia and I are most grateful."

"It is I who am grateful, Martin. You have brought me much joy and companionship, and I shall miss you."

"Then you must visit us in Luxembourg when we are resettled and give me the opportunity to be your host."

"Do come," Celia added, clasping my hand. "And you too, Lady Grace."

The thought of seeing Stefan again had not crossed my mind, and I felt uncomfortable with the idea. "Perhaps." My single word response appeared to sadden Celia, but I could not commit myself. As far as Florence, I held no doubt she would accept Doctor Reyer's invitation.

"Now give me a good tight hug," I said to Celia, holding out my arms. We embraced for a long time. Out of the corner of my eyes, I saw Martin give Florence a tender kiss on her cheek. Her eyes watered as she struggled with her farewells. After the emotional farewell, they climbed into the car, and our driver took them to the station. By tomorrow evening they would be home.

As I closed the door, Florence wiped her tears with her handkerchief. My heart swelled with affection. For the first time, I saw her as a woman who I understood rather than Benedict's domineering mother. No doubt we would rely upon one another in the years ahead and become increasingly close.

"You should visit them as soon as they are settled," I encouraged her, putting my arm around her shoulder. "It would be good for you."

"I don't know if that is wise," she responded, shaking her head. "Then I will only have to say goodbye again."

Curious as to the depth of her fondness toward Martin, I overstepped the boundaries between us out of sheer curiosity.

"Do you love him?"

"What?" She took a step back and scoffed at my question.

"Do you love Martin? It's a simple question, Florence, and I shall not feel any less of you if you possess such affection."

Florence's annoyance faded as she brought her hands together and held them. A slight blush filled her cheeks. "He asked me to marry him, but I turned down the proposal."

Her unexpected announcement made my mouth gape open in surprise. "Why?"

"Why?" She balked as if I should know the

answer.

"Is it because of his class?"

"No, of course not." She dismissed me, waving her hand as if I should go away. "How can I leave? My grandchildren need me. You need me."

"I would never, Florence, suggest you should sacrifice your happiness for my welfare. Benedict, as you know, has left me and you well provided for under the trust. My only responsibility here is to raise a son he would be proud to carry on and a beautiful daughter."

"Those responsibilities can be overwhelming for a mother on her own, and I shall not abandon you for my selfish pursuits." She walked toward the parlor. "The discussion has ended. I'm going for a strong cup of tea."

Florence dismissed me as she often did when the discussion had ended as far as she was concerned, and I did not pursue it. As kind as it had been for her to agree to help me in my new situation, her choice saddened me. Would I have done the same had Stefan asked me to marry him? The thought was ludicrous since my duties were to Stratton Park and Benedict's legacy.

As the months passed, nevertheless, letters arrived from Doctor Reyer to Florence on a weekly basis. Their goodbyes had not been permanent as Florence eagerly answered his correspondence as soon as it came. Martin had established his practice again, but he mentioned nothing about Stefan and his pursuits. If Martin had written anything, Florence would not share it with me. Naturally, my curious nature wished to know. When I thought of him meeting and loving another woman, my heart could not bear it.

CHAPTER 23

A Piece of the Puzzle

The flowers I had placed on my husband's grave a week ago had wilted from the heat of the summer. England had begun to heal from the war and so had I from the shock of Benedict's needless death. Percy and I often took flowers to his grave, and I told him only of his father's bravery. I would never convey the truth of Benedict's death to my children as I determined to keep his heroism in their hearts and minds.

After replacing the flowers and stepping back to look at the grave marker, Percy remained quiet, holding my hand. I wanted to confess my unfaithfulness to his departed spirit and ask for forgiveness. Inwardly I had spoken the words but found them difficult to articulate vocally.

"We should get back to grandmother." I gave him a slight tug of my hand to direct him to the house. He made no protest because he knew his afternoon snack would be waiting. Florence had fussed over Percy as if Benedict had returned as a child. As we approached the house, I saw an unknown vehicle. Not able to place its owner, I entered the foyer curious as to who had called upon us without notice.

"Go upstairs Percy and let Nanny Jane know you're back." My hand gave him an encouraging pat on the head.

"Yes, Mama."

He gave no cause to disobey and headed up the stairs. I heard voices in the parlor but could not discern whom they belonged to until I came closer to the doorway. As soon as the recognizable voice of Doctor Reyer met my hearing, I rounded the corner happy to see him. What I didn't expect was that Celia and Stefan would be with him. Shocked, I halted in my step.

"There she is," Doctor Reyer cheerfully announced. Stefan stood to his feet while Celia jumped up and came toward me with arms wide. She had grown into a beautiful young lady, but her familiar dimples remained in her cheeks as well as her wild curly hair.

"Grace!"

Immediately she grabbed me in an embrace that nearly knocked me off my feet. Happy to see her, I closed my eyes and gave her an affectionate hug in return. When she let go of me, I smiled at her.

"What are you doing here?"

"We came for a visit," she answered.

"Well, this is a surprise." I glanced at Florence who grinned mischievously. "Did you know they were coming?"

"Yes, I admit that I did, but they wanted to surprise you."

"Really." My brow lifted over my right eye as I found the courage to look at Stefan. The conflict and years had matured him. He flashed his beautiful smile and approached.

"It is good to see you, Lady Grace."

"And you," I replied, trying not to gush like a schoolgirl.

"Are you visiting for very long?" I sat in an empty chair when everyone returned to their seats, feeling like a fool in their presence.

"My son will be here for some time, but I shall be returning to Luxembourg with Celia in a fortnight."

His surprising answer caught me off guard, and I turned and looked at Stefan. "What do you mean you are staying?" My heart beat like a drum in my ears over the surprising announcement.

"I have been accepted at the University of Cambridge Medical School," he announced with an air of pride in his voice.

After realizing my mouth gaped open in astonishment, I sputtered like a fool. "Congrat— Congratulations. What excellent news."

"He wants to be like father," Celia announced with a sly grin.

"And what do you think of your brother being a surgeon?" I asked her out of curiosity.

"Oh, I think he will be tolerable, but I'm not sure if I've forgiven him for leaving Belgium." Celia flashed Stefan a disgruntled stare.

"Well, I'm sure he will return after his finishes his studies," I countered in a calm tone.

"I have made Celia no promises," Stefan replied.

My eyes shifted in his direction at the hopeful comment. Florence, who had remained quiet watching the interaction, suddenly interjected into the conversation.

"I've told Stefan that he is more than welcome to visit Stratton Park. Our home is open to him on the weekends and whenever he has the opportunity for a break between studies."

Shocked at her announcement, I could barely speak. A lump formed in my throat at the contemplation of Stefan visiting our household on a regular basis. The idea of being in constant proximity to him flushed my face. Suddenly I couldn't breathe. Embarrassed about my reaction, I rose to my feet.

"Please . . . please excuse me," I stammered. My eyes avoided everyone as I abruptly left the room, gasping for air. After walking into the foyer, I stood for a minute attempting to catch my breath as my anxiety choked the life out of me. I heard footsteps approach from behind and spun around to see Florence.

"I've upset you," she confessed. Her hand grabbed mine. "I should have told you beforehand they were coming."

"I'm shocked, frankly, and dislike like the idea of the lieutenant . . . I mean Stefan, staying here at Stratton Park. It makes me feel uncomfortable at the prospect of a single male being under our roof. What will our acquaintances think?" Florence squeezed my hand and tilted her head, appearing amused at my excuse. In a sympathetic tone, she answered.

"You should know, Grace, you have honored Benedict since his death and proven to me your heart did hold affection for him as your husband. Nevertheless, I'm a practical woman. You are young, the children need a father, and you deserve the chance to love and be loved."

"Are you insinuating that I'm in love with Stefan?"

"Well, I'm not blind, my dear. You have held him in high regard since the moment he arrived to recuperate in our home."

Unable to look at Florence in the eyes, I lowered my head in guilt.

"If the young man is determined to study at

Cambridge, he is welcome at Stratton Park as far as I'm concerned. If something grows between the two of you, then so be it. If not, it was never meant to be."

"You sound more like a matchmaker than a mother-in-law," I quipped. "You lecture me yet you refuse Doctor Reyer's advances."

Florence chuckled. "He's beginning to wear down my resolve. Truthfully, if I knew you were happy and well cared for, I would move to Belgium and be his wife. Celia needs a mothering influence at this precarious age of entering womanhood."

Instantly I felt guilty her happiness relied upon my ability to rekindle a relationship with Stefan. It made me wonder how much she knew about my former affections. Nevertheless, she stood here before me without condemnation but with encouragement.

"Am I interrupting anything?"

I jolted when I heard Stefan's voice. He stood a few feet away with a pleasing grin on his face and a twinkle in his gorgeous blue eyes.

"Not at all," Florence replied. "Why don't the two of you have a nice chat?"

As swiftly as she had arrived to join me in the foyer, Florence disappeared into the parlor. Stefan took two careful steps in my direction and then stopped. The reaction to his nearness sent a warm glow through my body. How could one man elicit such a response while doing absolutely nothing except standing there?

"I see we have stunned you with the news." He grinned sheepishly.

"Quite," I replied, trying to control my emotions. "I'm not sure what to think of it all."

"Think whatever you will, Grace. I am coming to Cambridge to study. That is my prime purpose," he replied.

"Well, I think it's wonderful you wish to follow in your father's footsteps."

"Before the war, I considered such a career path."

"You didn't mention it before." By all accounts, I had to admit I knew little about Stefan.

"Our time together had quickly passed and under the circumstances . . ." His grin faded. "Please accept my condolences over the death of your husband."

The subject of Benedict had entered our midst, resurrecting my guilt from the past. Stefan's tone convinced me of his sincerity. "Thank you. It was entirely unexpected, you know."

"Father conveyed to me he had returned from an overdue leave but had suffered emotional distress from duty."

"He came back for the birth of our daughter," I clarified, confused over Stefan's misconception of events.

"Birth of your daughter?" His eyes widened in surprise, and I knew exactly where his mind had taken him.

"Yes, after you both left, I discovered I was with child." He looked at me with a questioning gaze. "Her name is Amelia, and she looks very much like Benedict's family." Stefan's countenance relaxed as he exhaled a puff of air from between his lips.

"I see." He bowed his head. "Then I owe you congratulations as well."

Surprised Doctor Reyer had kept his promise of not telling Stefan, I did not feel compelled to say anything further.

"I have missed you," I confessed in a lowered voice. "There isn't a day that goes by that I don't think about what transpired . . ." I hesitated then spoke. "Nor do I regret it."

Our eyes met again, and he reciprocated his pleasure with a grin. "It was quite the improper dalliance under the circumstances, but I have never pushed the memory away either."

As we stood there staring at each other with unspoken thoughts, I became uncomfortable leaving the others alone.

"We should get back. It was foolish of me

excusing myself so awkwardly."

"I'm sure we'll have plenty of time to talk in the future," Stefan replied.

"Oh, I'm confident that we will," I agreed, lifting a teasing grin.

Perhaps I did have a future with the young and handsome Belgian surgeon-to-be. He had stolen my heart as a lieutenant, and I hoped he would reclaim it to bring healing of another sort.

As we walked into the parlor and everyone's eyes turned to us with noticeable approval, I believed the last piece of the puzzle had arrived to replace the one left empty by Benedict's death. Whatever final scene it would eventually create, I could only hope it would be one of peace and remain untouched by another war.

~The End~

Thank you for reading *Lady Grace*. To learn more about the research behind this story, visit my *Ladies of Disgrace Blog* at https://ladiesofdisgrace.wordpress.com/ for interesting articles and background information.

ABOUT THE AUTHOR

With Russian blood on my father's side and English on my mother's, I blame my ancestors for the lethal combination of my DNA that influences my stories. Tragedy and drama might be found between the pages, but I eventually give readers a happy ending.

I live in the beautiful, but rainy, Pacific Northwest. My hobby (more of an obsession) is researching my English ancestry and expanding my family tree. To keep the memory of my ancestors alive, I often use their names in my novels.

My usual genre is historical fiction with romantic elements and historical romance set in the Victorian and Edwardian eras. My books include:

- ❖ The Price of Innocence (Permanently Free) – Book One of the Legacy Series

- ❖ The Price of Deception – Book Two of the Legacy Series

- ❖ The Price of Love – Book Three of the Legacy Series

- ❖ The Price of Passion – Book Four of the Legacy Series

- ❖ The Legacy Series Box Set (Books 1-4)

- ❖ The Phantom of Valletta (Featured in The Sunday Times, Malta in 2010)

- ❖ Dark Persuasion (2012 Finalist in the USA Best Book Awards for Romance)

- ❖ A Portrait of Perfection (A Dark Gothic Tale of Love and Betrayal)

- ❖ A Christmas Oath (2015 Christmas Novelette)

- ❖ A Christmas Mission (2016 Christmas Novelette)

- ❖ Lady Isabella (Ladies of Disgrace)

- ❖ Lady Grace (Ladies of Disgrace)

- ❖ Lady Charlotte (Ladies of Disgrace)

Romance With a Kiss of Suspense, under the pen name of Nora Covington. Works to date include:

- ❖ Thorncroft Manor
- ❖ Whitefield Hall
- ❖ Blythe Court
- ❖ Romance With a Kiss of Suspense Box Set

Contemporary Romance:

❖ Conflicting Hearts, by J.D. Burrows -
  Contemporary Romance/Women's
  Fiction.

Sign up for my newsletter and author blog by visiting my official website.

http://vickihopkins.com